Jonna-Lynn Mandelb~~~

MW00874536

DAPHNE

and

THEKLA

outskirtspress
DENVER, COLORADO

Outskirts Press, Inc.
http://www.outskirtspress.com

ISBN: 978-1-4787-6476-2

Outskirts Press and the "OP" logo are trademarks belonging to Outskirts Press, Inc.

Preface

One of the basic requirements when I went to a church-affiliated college in the late 1960's was to take a course on the Old Testament and another on the New Testament. After graduation, I continued to read theology books and participate in various adult Bible study groups. While these activities were interesting, nothing sparked my curiosity like it did in 1992, when I presented seminars for the United Methodist Women's Schools of Mission on the topic of "Churches in Solidarity with Women." Both the preparation for teaching the seminars and the reactions of the participants in those classes left a lasting impression on me, prompting me to continue studying the lives of biblical women and the earliest years of Christianity.

The entire experience of studying and teaching was liberating because my understanding of the lives of biblical women previously had been very narrow. I am captivated by the strength and heroic acts of such little known women as Jael and Jephthath as well as female leaders from the first century of Christianity who are generally mentioned by name, but with limited information about their roles in the new faith. One woman who lived during the first decades after Jesus's life was Thekla (also spelled as Tekla, Tecla and Thecla). I first learned about her when I took the certification course prior to presenting the seminars on "Churches in Solidarity with Women." Thekla was mentioned briefly as someone who worked with Paul, but whose activities were not included in the New Testament. It was difficult to find information about her in the 1990's, but the availability of the internet made searches more feasible. It was easy to download and print the "Acts of Paul and Thecla." The more I looked and questioned sources about her life and times the more related information I found.

Some church leaders in the first centuries considered her story a mere legend, others felt that such a person simply may have existed. Early religious leaders feared the impact that Thekla's story might have on other women so they tried to minimize the circulation of the document, "The Acts of Paul and Thecla" and the shorter version called, "The Acts of Thecla." More recently, women theological scholars have given more credence to Thekla's story since some truth prompted the origin of the legends. At any rate, her story fascinates me and is presented to you in the following pages as an historical novel.

Concepts and phrases that were common during the first decades of Christianity are used throughout this book. At the time, the Holy Spirit and Holy Wisdom or Sophia were identified as female aspects of the Divine. For this reason, I use the pronouns "she" and "her" to refer to the Holy Spirit. Jesus taught in Aramaic which is a language open to a more flexible interpretation than many modern languages when translated. In Aramaic, Jesus was first identified as the Life-Giver and that term is used in the story that follows. These two concepts were minimized or lost over time as the church developed its organizational structure, theological underpinnings, and liturgy.

May your life be filled with love, joy, and peace as you discover Thecla.

JonnaLynn
August 4, 2015
Taos, NM

Prologue

I knew Abrax, Thekla's father, and through him came to know his daughter. From the first time we met, I was impressed with the poise and intelligence she possessed at such a young age. A strong friendship grew between us as she developed over the years into a remarkable individual.

Convinced that her story should be known by other women, I looked for ways to have it written properly by a professional. On Iconium's Street of the Scribes, there are so many stalls that I was sure one would be eager to accept this generous commission, but none considered it. Some even laughed at the idea of writing about a woman.

Perhaps I should have anticipated their reactions, since this Roman society in which I live is controlled exclusively by men and recognizes only those women classified as matriarchs, preferably with children. I think that's not much of a designation and reminds me of a brood mare. A single woman, regardless of her achievements, is viewed as a scandalous being and totally without merit to have any permanent record of her work. Perhaps they fear that other women will follow her as a role model. Staunchly undergirded by Roman law, every option possible prevents a woman from governing her own life much less living independently.

I turned to the spiritual leaders of the New Faith in the hope that they would see the value of recording Thekla's life to support their teachings and as a guide for women of the faith. They were as reluctant as the Roman scribes. Jewish laws keep women, for the most part, silent and hidden in their homes among their families. I looked into every possibility for a professional skilled enough to make an unbiased record about Thekla.

Although I had not been deeply involved in the New Faith, my friendship with Lectra, another believer of the New Faith, and observing how Thekla lived now led me to believe that it was consistently taught to others. I had assumed that there was an organized belief system for the New Faith, but gradually discovered that it was actually fraught with struggles from both within and without. In an effort to consolidate the tenets of their beliefs, the leaders often fought with each other to establish what was "true" about the life and teachings of their founder Jesus. Sometimes they denigrated fundamental elements of each other's views. While these squabbles arose among many of the disciples and apostles, the most controversial was Paul, Thekla's spiritual guide and mentor. The mere mention of Paul closed further discussion about writing her biography. In general, the leaders of the New Faith were more interested in disqualifying his work and distorting his teachings because he often defied social customs, especially regarding marriage. There was an element of fear that the way he provoked controversy led to more condemnation from authorities.

However, I could not rest until Thekla's story had been recorded. Her life and actions are too important to allow them to disintegrate into the dust of time. With no other alternative available, I have decided to make it my purpose for the remaining years of my life to record the truth about Thekla, called an apostle by Paul.

May the reading of these pages bring you blessings,

Daphne

Storm and Fire

The day that had started with such beautiful weather now bore down on Iconium with intense wrath as it approached midday; it seemed like the gods had been offended. The servants ran to bring in the pillows and carpets from the courtyard as a mixture of rain and hail battered anything outside. Water poured off the roof into the courtyard filling my small pool and then drained into the cistern for future use. I watched in disbelief as the winds shredded curtains before I could close the doors and windows. Such ferocity had not been seen in the region for decades, if ever. Finally, the storm passed, the winds calmed and the skies lightened. We heard someone calling at the front entrance of the villa.

I was the closest to the door and was the first to respond. It was swollen with moisture and resisted my efforts to pull it open. When the door jamb suddenly yielded, I fell against the wall. A young woman, cut and bruised, stood before me naked except for the tarp from an awning she had wrapped around her. Shocked by the appearance of this vagrant, it took me a moment to recognize Thekla. The typical tilt of her head and hint of a smile whenever she felt at ease verified her identity beyond question. Noting the cuts and bruises on her arms, I gasped. I pulled her into the villa, helping her into the spare room while calling for warm water, hot broth and clothes as we walked. My mind reeled with questions. I was glad to take her in, but for a fleeting moment, I wondered why she had not gone to her own home.

A quick glance around the room assured me that it was ready for an unexpected guest. Simple, pale blue curtains covered the window, muting the harsh daylight. The bed was ample and the linens were fresh. There were few other adornments in the room since it was rarely used. The servants brought in a basin of water, ointments, and bandages, and a tray of food. I knew that Thekla could be comfortable here and undisturbed by the household activities.

As I guided Thekla into the bedroom, she stopped and said, "Before we do anything, I need to send word to my servants, Pallas and Acca, to pack everything immediately to go to the country villa. Maybe Acca can send me some clothes. I also need to meet with Gauis the magistrate as soon as possible."

Puzzled by her unusual requests, my concern for Thekla deepened. "My servants will carry your messages. When you're ready, tell me what has happened."

Thekla's lips curved into a gentle smile. "You must be one of the few in the city who doesn't know what's been going on." She took a deep breath and began to talk quietly.

"About a week ago, Onesiphorus, our neighbor across the street, had a houseguest who talked to anyone who gathered there about a new faith way. My window was opposite the place where they met every day. Soon, I was engrossed in his teachings about this way of living in love with faith in an unseen God. He also said that, despite the Roman law that requires women to marry, those called to this life could remain single and be well received in a life after death. I was captivated by his words and didn't want to miss anything he said."

Her voice was not much more than a whisper so I leaned closer to her as she spoke. "Occupied with Paul's teaching I didn't realize that, my mother Theokleia had decided to finalize my marriage contract with Thamyris. She tried to get me to leave my room and when I wouldn't yield to her commands to prepare for my marriage, she got angry. She made arrangements through Thamyris to have Paul arrested, immediately. That night, I left our villa and bribed guards along the way with some of my jewelry so that I could see him in prison."

Thekla pursued information on her own rather than accept someone else's claims. I could understand her desire to meet this man face to face to question his teachings, but this level of boldness startled me and seemed out of character. I masked my reaction and chose my words carefully. My maid and I finished cleaning her cuts and pulled a clean, soft tunic over her head. She winced as the cloth rubbed against the wounds.

I leaned against my chair and said, "Paul must be a very remarkable man."

She shook her head and said, "It's not him as a person as much as it is his teachings, which struck something deep inside me. I was determined to understand more about living a life of genuine love. He teaches that it is not required for women to marry. The possibility of remaining single coincided with the hopes I had for my life. A new sense of awareness and purpose began to unfold deep inside."

"When did you see the teacher?" I asked. It was hard to grasp all that she was saying. Her story was so strange that I even wondered if she was ill.

"It must have been the night before last. Everything went so fast that my days and nights got mixed up. Although I'd only heard him speak while I was seated in the window of my room, I felt compelled to meet him. By bribing the guards with my jewerly, I was able to stay with Paul until he went before the judge, who ordered him to be flogged and expelled from Iconium. Immediately after his trial, I was brought before the judge because I had stayed the night with Paul in his cell. The jaliors told wild stories, saying that I threw myself at Paul and clung to him as if I were his lover." She glanced at me with a wide-eyed look of disbelief. "During the court proceedings, Theokleia emphasized the fact that I refused to have the marriage contract with Thamyris finalized and convinced the judge that unless I was severely punished, other young women also would try to avoid marriage. She said I was a risk to society as long as I lived. She exchanged a penetrating look with the judge who announced that I would be burned to death in the market square as soon as arrangements could be made."

Shocked by what Theokleia had done as well as the brutal punishment, I gasped. "I had no idea. Couldn't you get a message to me?
Perhaps I could have helped somehow."

Thekla shook her head. "I'd used everything I had with me to bribe
the household guards and jailors. Then, they sent my servant Acca away
when I was taken to court. Besides, I believe that Theokleia had spoken
with the judge regarding the punishment before he saw me. She stands
to gain everything from my father's inheritance if I die."

I rubbed Thekla's cold hands and said, "Over the years she has
learned a lot of secrets and can wield power over many city leaders.
Your father spoke about the ways she manipulated people. She even
promised the temples and gods huge gifts if they would guarantee that
her baby would be born a boy." I knew her mother's actions had gone
beyond merely trying to sway the gods, because Abrax had told me
how his wife had tried to bribe the midwife to kill the baby as soon
as it was born if it were a girl. If Thekla knew about her efforts with
the midwife, she never mentioned them and I saw no reason to say
anything now.

Thekla nodded. "At home, I made it a point to avoid Theokleia
whenever I could, especially since the epidemic and the deaths of my
father and my brother Agapetos, but this experience teaches me that
there's no easy way to avoid her extensive network. I can count on
some of my father's friends, but no one else."

"Where did they take you after the trial was over?" I asked.

"Back to the prison until the pyre could be prepared. It was supposed to be a spectacle to entertain the citizens. There were flute
players and jugglers as they stacked the wood in the center of the
market square. Today at noon, I was to be burned to death." Thekla
had been very pale when she arrived and her normally rosy cheeks
still were not regaining their color despite being wrapped in blankets
as she talked.

"How can you be so calm about this?" I asked, astonished at her composure as she related the events. She sat on the edge of the couch with her hands folded in her lap. She didn't move a muscle as she talked. Her voice was flat without a hint of anger and her face showed no expression to match her words. I couldn't decide whether she had other physical injuries or if she was in shock from her mother's effort to destroy her.

"As I listened to Paul, I gained new insight about my life in a totally new way. I know that we are born to love and care for others regardless of how they treat us. People act in the only way they know how, even when it harms us. Although I don't like it, I finally understood that Theokleia can't help but be who she is. The only person I'm responsible for is me. I have only my own life to live in love, as Jesus, the founder of this faith-way taught. He could have avoided being crucified, but didn't in order to fulfill his teaching. He gave up his life for love of others. Paul could have challenged the judge in court, instead he told them about this new way of living. Knowing how these people of the new faith handle dire situations makes me want to be like them." Her last statement was made with such firm conviction that I had no doubt about her pursuit of the new beliefs. Only now, as she spoke about Paul's teachings, did her face grow animated and some color returned to her cheeks. Questions flashed through my thoughts, but I limited my comments. "How did you end up here?"

"I was stripped of my clothes and led to the pyre. Even after I was bound to the stake, people jeered and threw rotten food and stones at me. The sky was clear and a light breeze helped the flames to catch. Smoke swirled around me making it difficult to breathe, and tears covered my cheeks. The crowd roared. Suddenly, the wind rose and a black thundercloud settled over the square. Rain and sleet pelted the ground. People ran for cover as the wind intensified, tearing off any loose awning or mat.

She sipped some warm spiced wine and with a deep sigh continued telling me what had happened. "Thunder rolled like huge copper drums and lightning flashed; I could hardly see through the torrents. Finally, when the storm passed, there was profound silence. A warm breeze enveloped me and I felt profoundly that I was loved as the person I am. I didn't want that moment to end. A sudden chill seized me and I realized that the market was empty, my bonds had loosened in the rain and the fire was out. I grabbed the first cloth I could find and started to walk. Knowing Theokeia's role in this, I couldn't go home, so I came to you." At that point, Thekla's voice faltered and she wept.

"Rest until we get the replies from your messages." I embraced her, then shook out another heavier blanket and covered her. She sank into the bed exhausted and closed her eyes.

I stood outside her room reflecting on all that she had said. It was an incredible tale. If I didn't know her well, or about her mother's actions in the past, I would have doubted much of her story. For as long as I had known her, Thekla had always been truthful, even when it would have been easier for her to lie. Besides, there was a veracity in the way she spoke that compelled me to listen receptively to her description of all that had happened.

As the sky darkened with sunset, Gauis and I sat in the living room sipping wine. This was the first time he had come to my home. He and I first met when Abrax was widowed and needed a companion to accompany him to formal functions in the city. I had not seen him since Abrax's second marriage to Theokleia.

Even when Gauis was seated it was easy to see that he was a tall man. Dark brown curls framed a kind face. Gaius had been Abrax's best friend. I knew that in his role as a city magistrate, Gaius had explained the settlement from Abrax's estate to Thekla and Theokleia after his sudden death from the plague. The terms of the will would have been different had her younger brother Agapetos survived the disease and been old enough to handle the responsibility, but he died within a day of his father. I assumed that Gaius had assisted Abrax to divide his estate equally between Thekla and Theokleia. Thekla now owned his country property and everything from her wing in the city villa, including the servants who cared for her. There must have been some financial settlement between the two women so that they could maintain the properties, but I never heard about it.

I had given a lot of thought to what Thekla told me about her recent arrest and punishment. One thing nagged at me: I wondered what role Thamyris had played in these events. Was he manipulated by Theokleia like so many others? Gauis was the only person I could ask who could offer some insight about the young man.

"Abrax never mentioned that he was arranging a marriage to Thekla. Since he discussed so many things with me, I was very surprised when Thekla told me about the contract after her father died. Do you know how the betrothal between Thamyris and Thekla came about?" I asked.

At first Gaius remained siltent, staring at his hands. "I recall the day very clearly because Abrax's actions surprised me. Thamyris, despite being young is developing a good reputation for leadership in the community. Abrax, Thamyris and I spent quite a bit of time together on various civic and business endeavors. Since Thamyris is my nephew, I expected Abrax to discuss such a serious matter with me before arranging a betrothal for Thekla. Thamyris admires Thekla's beauty, but he's not attracted to her. I know that Thamyris is committed to a young man and has lived with him for several years."

Among Greeks and Romans, it was not unusual for young men to have male lovers as long as they were discreet and established their own household with a wife and children. The news about Thamyris's relationship did not surprise me, but made me wonder how committed he would be to a marriage. I knew that some men remained very close to their male companions despite setting up a household with their wives. I often wondered whether the women were barren or whether they were neglected by their husbands. I felt deep sadness for Thekla if she ended up married to this man.

Gaius continued. "As I prepared the legal document, I thought Thamyris might reject the marriage contract. Both he and Abrax signed it without much discussion. Much later, I found out that my sister and her husband had been pressuring him to marry and establish a family. Thamyris is very astute about social requirements, making me think that he might have planned some other option for him and his lover to manage their relationship. Of course, to be respected in business and pursue any role in the city's governance, he would have to live up to social expectations."

It was hard to hear Gauis's description of the betrothal because the whole thing seemed out of character for the Abrax I knew. I loosened the palla around my shoulders and thought about all that Gaius had said before making any comment. "It seems so complicated. Abrax never hinted to me that he was anxious to settle Thekla's future and I'm sure he never mentioned it to her. As determined as she is to be independent, she would have told me."

Gaius nodded. "I couldn't figure it out either. Since then, I've wondered whether Theokleia was plotting against her daughter in such a way that made Abrax want to guarantee that Thekla would be out of the household and safe."

There was a comfortable silence between us as we thought about Abrax and his actions.

When Thekla joined us, Gauis's eyes widened as he noted the bruises on her face and arms. At first glance, Thekla appeared delicate, but I knew the drape of her palla hid well-muscled arms. She had an athletic build that would have suited her well had she been raised in Sparta where naked athletes of both sexes were admired. Her chestnut hair was pulled away from her face and revealed the graceful angles of her cheeks and chin. Despite the rigors of the past few days, her beauty was apparent.

"Daphne told me how you escaped. I'm sorry that I didn't know. Perhaps I could have intervened on your behalf."

"I'm sure that you were kept uninformed deliberately so that no one could represent me." Although she looked better than when she had arrived, dark circles around her eyes revealed the extent of her exhaustion as she took a seat near him. "But that is over and, with your help, I will make some new arrangements. I need to move my servants and other possessions from the city villa into the country home as soon as possible. Theokleia is vengeful and will not treat them fairly because they have always cared for me. I've sent them a message to pack immediately and be ready to leave in the morning. Can you arrange for a wagon to get them away?" Her voice, though soft, was firm as she explained her needs.

"Thekla, that's no problem. I'll go to the villa first, then come by Daphne's and pick you up."

"Oh, no. If there is a search for me, the first place Theokleia would send men is the country villa." Thekla shook her head vigorously. "Eventually, I'll join them, but not tomorrow. There are some other things I must do first."

"Surely I can help you with those things if you just tell me what's needed," Gauis said as he searched her face for a clearer understanding.

"Gaius, the less you know about my plans now, the easier you will be able to deal with Theokleia and the others. You won't know where I've gone or what I'm doing. If, for some reason, you must reach me, please leave the message with Daphne and I'll reply as soon as I can."

Gaius glanced at me with an inscrutable expression. I had been his best friend Abrax's hetaera. Under normal circumstances, a man's family had no contact with his hetaera. With Theokleia's rejection of her daughter, Thekla's life had been far from normal. I suspected that Gauis didn't know that Abrax asked me to help his daughter prepare for her role in society.

"Thekla and I have known each other for years. Out of my

friendship for her and for her father, I will assist her in any way I can. Feel free to contact me as you need to."

Gaius raised his eyebrows. I gave him a reassuring smile. "When Abrax died, I retired as a hetaera. I had no need to keep working and lost the desire to be deeply involved in a social life that led nowhere. My purpose now is to be a friend to Thekla."

Even as I spoke, the situation seemed unreal. I still harbored doubts and questions about everything that was happening, but I knew I had to help Thekla regardless.

Thekla and Gaius continued to discuss plans for the country home. Repairs had been neglected since Abrax's death. The caretaker needed funds to proceed and expand the house to accommodate Acca, Thekla's maid and Pallas, her tutor. Gaius made several suggestions and planned to take some of her money with him so that the work could be started immediately.

My servant came to light the oil lamps. It was nearly evening when they finished their discussion. As Gaius stood up, we accompanied him to the door. He turned to Thekla once more, "Please don't hesitate to let me assist you whenever possible. It is very difficult for a single woman to manage on her own."

The day had been demanding in many ways, but as tired as I was, sleep eluded me. At first, I reviewed everything that Thekla had said and all that she had planned with Gaius. Tired of that pointless exercise, I closed my eyes and suddenly saw Abrax's face. How often I had wished that life could have been different for us, but I couldn't allow myself to daydream about what might have been had we been able to marry.

I smiled into the darkness thinking about the first time Thekla came to my villa with her father. Abrax and I exchanged our customary warm greetings speaking Galatian to include Thekla. Without thinking, we switched to Greek. When I bent down to the child's level, Thekla responded to me properly in Greek. What a delightful surprise to discover the girl's ability to switch from one language to the other unprompted. Abrax beamed with pride.

Of course, I was drawn to the precocious child and welcomed her with a warm smile and gentle hug. "Would you go to the courtyard and see if the refreshments are ready for us?"

She nodded, eager to do something, and ran to the garden.

Soon after her birth, Abrax came to me and said, "Theokleia wanted to destroy her at birth despite the fact that she was perfect in every way. After losing my first wife and infant son in childbirth, I cannot grasp Theokleia's thinking." Abrax shook his head, not expecting an answer, but needing the relief of telling someone. "Fortunately, I have good servants who will care for Thekla and let me know if her mother ever tries to harm her."

From then on, he kept me up to date on anything that affected Thekla.

For years, I had been a slave in Greece and returned to Iconium after being given my freedom and becoming well established as a *hetaera*. I returned to my homeland a wealthy woman. Once I met Abrax, I lost the desire to continue working. As my clients moved away, I did not replace them. By the time Abrax brought Thekla to see me, he was my only client.

After that first visit, we met regularly. I spent hours with Thekla and grew to love the girl. Soon after she turned ten years old, I showed her how to fix her hair and use cosmeta. "In a few years, you will marry and have a servant to do this for you, but it is good for you to know how to curl your hair and add color to eyes and face," I said, as I wound a strand of Thekla's dark hair around my finger.

"What if I don't want to marry?" Thekla asked. "Can't I have my own home like you?"

I remained quiet for several minutes as I continued to style her hair. I knew that there was some wisdom in the child's words because my life of capture and slavery before becoming a hetaera was an example of life's unexpected twists. I chose my words with care. "Life is full of surprises so it is hard to plan for the future. Women are expected to marry and have children."

"Can't I choose to be on my own?" Thekla persisted with her question.

I didn't answer her at first as I tried to decide how much I should tell her about my background. "I didn't choose this life for myself, but I am happy now." Thekla looked confused. "Let me tell you how it happened. My parents lived in the town of Daphne, not far from here and we had a villa much larger than this one with extensive fields. I was studying Greek and Latin. We weren't aware of fighting in our region, but without warning troops attacked our town. I was taken from my home and sold as a slave."

"Did you escape?" asked Thekla with wide eyes.

"No." I tucked a curl into the braid around Thekla's head and continued. "Everyone they captured was marched to Athens and sold as a slave. I was kept there for several years until my owner died. He was a kind man and in his will he set all of his slaves free. The first day of my freedom, I wandered around the streets exploring the town until late in the afternoon when I realized that I had no home, no place to sleep. I followed a hetaera who was too old to have many clients and she let me stay with her. In return for helping her, she taught me all that I know from how to dress to entertaining men."

Watching every expression on my face, Thekla interrupted and asked, "But how did you get to Iconium?"

"I longed to come home to Galatia, so when Cassandra, my teacher died, I chose to return."

A New Beginning

Morning broke with clear skies and brilliant sunshine. It was hard to believe the amount of destruction wreaked by the storm the day before. Fortunately, my villa sustained little structural damage and required only minor repairs outside. My courtyard garden, however, would take months to prune and replant. At least the small fish in my pool were unaffected and easily swam around the debris that had fallen into the water. The air was heavy with the scent of torn flowers and I inhaled deeply. Then, I crumbled some bread from breakfast into crumbs for the fish. How I delighted in their beauty and graceful movement. Thekla's approaching footsteps brought me out of my reverie me and I patted the cushions for her to sit down.

"You look well rested. Do your bruises bother you?"

Thekla kissed me on the cheek before taking her seat. "I feel so much better. Thank you for taking me in yesterday."

"You are like a daughter to me. I will always support and help you any way I can." I scrutinized her face for any lingering sign of pain or stress.

"The worst is over, I think. As soon as I know Acca and Pallas have left for the country villa, I'll be ready to move on. Gaius will send a messenger once he's been able to get them out of the city. Since Theokleia doesn't know that I'm still alive, he will need to tell her that she has no claim on my servants or our possessions." Thekla poured herself fresh juice and inhaled its citrus scent before taking a sip, then tore her flatbread into several smaller pieces before eating them, a habit from childhood that reappeared whenever she was preoccupied.

I was very glad that I didn't have to be the one to give Theokleia any news about her daughter. Abrax had often told how his wife loved to spend money on luxurious gems and other cosmeta. I knew the loss of Thekla's share of his estate would incrrease her fury over the unintended results of her conniving.

"Do you think Theokleia will search for you once she knows that you escaped being burned?" I asked. I recalled another conversation with Abrax when Thekla was six years old. Despite his walk to my villa, his anger was still white hot. He told me that Theokleia had hit their daughter so hard that she left the imprint of her hand on the child's face. Her behavior made him decide not to have any more children with her. I asked why he didn't divorce her and force her to return to her home, and he said he wanted to keep his family together for his son's sake. He would preserve the relationship Theokleia had with Agapetos while being vigilant for Thekla's safety.

Thekla's voice brought me back to the present.

"What more can Theokleia do? She has no idea that I know anyone in Iconium and doesn't realize that I might come to you for help. My father kept our relationship with you secret as if it were a completely different life. In addition, yesterday as I walked here, the damage in the city seemed to be extensive. People will be intent on repairing their stalls and securing their wares rather than looking forward to a few hours of entertainment as they watch someone burn. Theokleia, too, will be busy repairing her villa. By the time she decides to chase after me, I hope to be gone from Iconium."

I nodded. "Based on what my servants tell me about the damage near us, I agree with you, but never underestimate your mother. Your father knew that she had an extensive network of informers and wielded considerable power behind the scenes in Iconium. He always kept that in mind as he went about his business negotiations." Looking at her intently, I wanted to be sure she understood that she might not be out of danger.

Thekla gave my hand a gentle squeeze. "I cannot stay with you without starting rumors. When men come to your house, people understand, but having a young woman living with you for an extend-ed period may cause them to think that you are training another he-taera. I must find Paul as soon as possible and learn more from him."

"But . . ." I was at a loss for words.

"Paul's teachings reach deep inside me and compel me to learn all that I can. During the storm, I never felt alone. There was a divine Spirit with me. She was telling me that my work had just begun and my first step was to find the apostle." As Thekla spoke her face radi-ated joyful confidence.

"I have never known such assurance from any other deity. Our gods and goddesses gave me no response whenever I tried to commit myself to them. The priestesses rebuffed my questions and said that only one who belonged to the temple could pursue such knowledge. Although my experience with Paul's teachings have been for only a few days, I know that this is my purpose."

Seeing the set of her jaw and knowing that once Thekla's mind was set, she could not be deterred from the path she chose, I said, "I have only one request, Thekla, and that is for you to stay here until your cuts and bruises have healed."

"Thank you for your concern, but I have to get going now before people are aware that I'm here. And at this point, any delay could mean that I lose the chance of finding him."

I knew I could not influence her determination and silenced the nagging questions that bothered me about her involvement with this man and his teachings. "Let me arrange an enclosed litter to get you out of Iconium. Keep it as long as you can, both for the sake of healing and for your safety." My tone was gentle, but firm.

As a young woman, I had tried to pursue my independence and Cassandra had guided me. So I understood a little bit of Thekla's ur-gency to move ahead with her plans.

Since the best time to leave Iconium was when the gates were most crowded and the soldiers more concerned with keeping people moving than who was leaving, Thekla decided to remain one more night with me. She timed her departure for the early morning when merchants and villagers thronged the gates for entrance.

For her journey, Thekla selected the plainest clothes she had and a pair of comfortable, well-worn sandals from the clothes that Acca had sent. Everything else would stay with me until she sent for it. The tension on her face eased as the old tunic slid over her skin. Even a simple dress could not obscure her beauty. She didn't wear any jewelry and carried a modest amount of money hidden in her belt and the hem of her tunic. My eyes filled with tears as we said good-bye, and I held on to her as long as I could. I felt torn with her moving into the unknown. Would I see her again?

"I'll send a messenger to you whenever I can, especially when I know I'm on my way back to Iconium." Filled with excitement and anxious to see Paul, Thekla was eager to be on her way.

When she was no longer in sight, I walked back into my home. Doubts assailed me. Had I done enough to protect andguide her? I asked my servants to be aleert for any new rumors about Thekla.

A Visitor

Two days later, I was working in the garden, tending plants that had survived the storm when my maid said, "A Roman matron has come to see you, mistress."

"Are you sure she didn't get lost and come to the wrong villa? A proper Roman matron would never associate with a hetaera," I said. Although we were highly respected among most elite men, our existence was ignored by society women.

My maid shook her head. "The lady said that she needed to see you about Thekla."

My stomach knotted with worry. I called for a basin so that I could wash and had refreshments sent to the lady waiting in the living room. With my palla carefully arranged over my shoulders, I hoped I looked more presentable.

The Roman matron was sitting at ease in the living room sipping fruit juice from a chalice she held with a small, delicate hand. She was not an especially attractive woman, with a long narrow face and prominent nose. Her brown hair was unadorned, but neatly arranged in a series of braids wound around her head. However, she smiled when she saw me and her face was almost beautiful, projecting sincerity with its warmth. Her countenance relieved some of the anxiety that had grown inside when I heard my maid say Thekla's name.

"Welcome to my home. I have never had a matron visit me before." A flush of embarrassment colored my cheeks.

"My name is Lectra; I am Onesiphorus's wife and we are Thekla's neighbors. Paul was staying with us when Thekla heard him speak."

Her voice was gentle and easy to listen to. I nodded, but didn't interrupt her.

"Thekla asked me to have a letter delivered to you, but I thought it would be better if I brought it myself," Lectra said.

"I'm glad to meet you, but I'm sorry to put you to the trouble of coming here," I said taking the scroll from her outstretched hand.

"For us who follow Paul's teaching about Jesus, we find no difference between men and women, slave and free. He says that we are free from any social bondage based on Jesus's teaching that God loves us all regardless of our status in life. That you're known as a hetaera does not prevent me from visiting you." Lectra's eyes twinkled.

What an amazing person. Few upperclass women would dare to associate with a hetaera at the risk of having scandalous rumors spread about her. "Tell me how you met Thekla."

"When we became believers, my husband and I decided that our home would be open to all who follow the way of Jesus. Some call it a house church. We care for the believers here and those traveling through Iconium, like Paul. After the judge sentenced him to be beaten and thrown out of the city, our family took Paul to a cave we own in the next village. There we were able to treat his wounds and allow him to recover. He told us about Thekla's arrest and we knew that she was to be burned. We prayed for her, that she would be delivered."

"When did you see her? How is she?" I couldn't keep quiet. I had to know if Thekla was all right.

Lectra gave a slight nod and smiled. "We left Paul and Thekla in the cave yesterday morning. When she arrived in the village, she met my oldest son, Zeno in the village market as he was buying food for us. We could hardly believe it when we saw her. Our prayers were answered beyond our expectation. Although we wanted to stay with them longer, Paul asked us to come home and continue to care for the believers here. That's when Thekla asked if I could get a letter to you."

"Thank you very much for bringing the scroll and telling me that Thekla is safe and with Paul. She is like a daughter to me. When she found herself alone in the square after the storm put out the fire, she came here. I wanted her to stay longer, but she insisted that she had to follow Paul before she lost the chance of finding him." I heard my comments and was surprised at myself for claiming Thekla as if she were my daughter.

Lectra listened carefully, then said, "May I ask how you came to meet Thekla?"

Despite the fact that Lectra had no qualms about my profession, I hesitated to acknowledge it and my relationship with Thekla's father. Lectra smiled in a way that encouraged me to speak freely. I felt no condemnation from her. "I was her father's hetaera," I began. "Over the years we became very close friends. When his first wife died, he asked me to marry him, but that would never have worked in Iconium. It would have ruined his reputation and his business. When Thekla was born, his second wife did not want her so Abrax had to make special arrangements for her to be cared for in his household. As she grew up, he noticed that her behavior was not being molded for the role of a society matron. He came to me for help when she was seven years old. At first, I refused because I didn't want her to be damned for associating with a hetaera. But, we could find no other solution, so I guided her as she grew up. We have known each other for several years and have become very close, especially after the death of her father."

"Although we live across the street, we had no social contact with her family. I had no idea what Thekla's life was like," said Lectra. "I can't imagine what it would have been like for her." Lectra looked sad and puzzled.

I said, "Thekla couldn't return to her home after the storm because her mother was the one who had demanded that she be burned."

Lectra leaned away as I spoke and her eyes opened wide. "It's wonderful that she has such a good friend like you."

We chatted briefly about current events in Iconium, then Lectra rose to leave. "Daphne, please feel free to visit us. I will be sure to let you know whenever I have any news of Thekla and Paul."

"Thank you. I'm so grateful that you came to see me and for bringing Thekla's letter."

My favorite spot in the garden offered me seclusion and silence, so I went there to read Thekla's letter. As I opened the scroll, I remembered how her father had wrestled with the decision to allow her to learn to write. He didn't want her trained as a scribe, but she was so eager to learn that he found it hard to refuse any opportunity for her. She was an apt student of languages and could read easily in Galatian, Latin or Greek. Although Abrax had thought that she would never need to write, he recognized her thirst for knowledge. How glad I am that she learned, since she could write exactly what she wanted to say without having to pay a professional who might change the intent of her message.

Dearest Daphne,

Thank you for all your help, especially with the litter. I decided to stop at the first village to see if I could find out whether Paul had been there. Lectra will have told you how I met her son and stayed with them in the cave. How wonderful it was to see them all and hear them talk about the life of Jesus and his way to live with love and forgiveness. It's made a big difference to me and the way I feel about Theokleia and Thamyris.

Paul is still recovering from being beaten by the soldiers. This gives us more time for me to learn about Jesus. We will stay here one or two more days before going to Antioch.

Whenever I have the opportunity, I will send you another letter. I know that Paul stays in contact with Onesiphorus so you may also receive news of our travels through him.

I send you my love.

Thekla.

I dropped Thekla's letter on the cushion next to me and gazed at the fish swimming in my tiny pool while my thoughts drifted in many directions. How could she be so convinced of this stranger's words? She professed such deep faith in a totally new set of values that could be viewed as antisocial in the Roman society. How could anything good come of this pursuit?

Thekla's regard for gods and spirits was incomprehensible to me. Long ago, I had given up any reliance on gods and goddesses. They were only clay figures made by artisans in the market. Even if I had been drawn to temple rituals and feasts, I would have been sent away from most because I was a hetaera. Their rules were devised by people and offered no comfort or guidance for me.

I knew from my experience that there is no way to control one's life. It would unfold in a good or bad way regardless of what plans had been proposed. My parents' dreams for me were much different than my life turned out. When I was a child at home, I willing participated in the rituals my parents chose. But, regardless of my sincere worship of the gods, my family was destroyed. I realized that the gods didn't care how faithful or generous we'd been to them. So I ignored them and tried to live my life with kind regard for most people and animals because my experiences taught me that most would respond to me with kindness, too.

This experience with Thekla baffled me. I couldn't imagine hearing someone speak and being to captivated by his words that I had to drop everything and follow him.

Lectra's Invitation

Weeks passed without further news of Thekla's travels. I tried not to worry about her, but concerns about her well-being often surfaced just before I fell asleep. Sometimes my imagination ran wild with speculation that Theokleia might still try to destroy her. According to Abrax, Thekla's beauty surpassed that of her mother and Theokleia did not tolerate rivals. When Abrax was alive, he could protect Thekla, but with his death there was no restraint on Theokleia. Recent events showed that she would do anything she wanted to eliminate her only daughter. Thekla's rapid departure from Iconium seemed to be the safest choice for her after all.

When Lectra's invitation to visit her home was delivered, I was both relieved and nervous since I had never made a social call to a Roman household. Clients always came to see me, or they sent for me to attend an official function with them.

I took special care in choosing a modest toga and matching palla. With my hair in a simple braid coiled around my head, I used no cosmeta and wore no jewelry. Pausing at the mirror, my altered reflection startled me. Slight blemishes on my skin were exposed, something I never allowed when I was working. My hair style was so simple that I felt the least bit uneasy going outside my home. Surely no one would guess that I'd been a hetaera all my life.

The distance to Lectra's villa provided a pleasant walk through my neighborhood and then the upper class section. Fruit trees were in blossom, filling the air with a light fruity scent. Passing through the streets I thought about how Abrax and Thekla had come this way to visit me. As I reached the intersection of the cross street for Onesiphorus's house, I paused and examined the ostentatious villa on the main thoroughfare where Thekla had grown up. Several fluted columns flanked the entrance where a guard stood by the door. Urns filled with plants were carefully arranged next to each column. Judging from the way the building extended along the side street toward Onesiphorus and Lectra's villa, the place that Abrax had built years ago for his family was extensive. I recalled how he said he had hoped for many children, but after the death of his first wife and baby during childbirth, he was deeply grateful for Thekla and her brother Agapetos.

I pulled my gaze away and continued walking toward Lectra's villa. Whe I arrived, I was surprised to see that there were only two fluted columns at the front door and no guard. The entrance seemed wide open so that anyone could enter. There was no adornment on the exterior, just a simple paved path that I followed. Someone noticed my approach and came outside to meet me.

"Welcome. You must be Daphne. We've been watching for you. Please come with me."

The youth resembled Lectra in the way he smiled and I wondered if he might be one of her sons. His smile seemed genuine and I began to relax.

We walked through the atrium to a courtyard with a small fountain in one corner and a few potted plants. Small groups of people, mostly women, were seated together. The waterfall added background music to their conversations. Some appeared to be sewing while others worked on a small project that I couldn't discern. Everyone seemed to be at ease and content. Finally, I spotted Lectra near the fountain.

"Thank you for bringing Daphne to me, Simmias." Lectra gave him a quick hug and turned to me. "Welcome to our home. Simmias is the younger of our two sons. Eventually, you will meet Zeno, too." Lectra gestured to the cushions where she sat.

I took my place next to her. "I was glad to receive your invitation. This is the first time I've been invited to a private home. Is there a special event today?"

Lectra laughed. "No, this is our normal household. Many of these women are widows and live with us. Others come to visit them and we always have time to share our understanding of Paul's teachings. I could see that you were puzzled when I said that we opened our home to believers, so I decided to invite you so that you could see for yourself."

"What an interesting group of people." As I looked around it seemed that some had been slaves because they bore the scars of severe punishment. Their clothes varied from very simple tunics and shawls to more elaborate togas and pallas. I realized that I fit in with the clothes that I'd chosen to wear.

"We all share a common faith in the life of Jesus and believe that we should live according to his teachings as Paul has told us. We have no distinctions, whether someone is a slave, a master, a soldier, widowed, or a young woman. We are all equal before God," she said. Lectra scanned the courtyard and continued, "While the villa belongs to our family, we all share whatever resources we have. The women in the far corner are sorting grain that was given to us by a man who always comes when Paul is here. Others are sewing for their own needs or for someone else. We are usually busy with something to help the people who come to us. A few women are in the kitchen preparing food. Skills and resources are shared which makes it possible for us to live together."

It amazed me to sit with Lectra and feel completely at ease. When I left my villa, I had been mentally rehearsing a gracious way to leave if I became too uncomfortable during my visit. What a surprise to be welcomed here without any probing questions or stares. I felt no pressing need to get away, as I had anticipated.

Lectra added, "Daphne, it's like this every day unless we plan a special feast or have a visitor like Paul."

Speechless, I could only smile.

Simmias came over carrying a scroll that he handed to his mother. "Did you want this?"

"Oh, yes. Thank you." Lectra turned to me and said, "I meant to have this with me to give it to you when you arrived.

I glanced at the writing on the outer surface and recognized Thekla's script.

Lectra continued, "They were in Lystra for several days. Paul sent a brief message to us. He's impressed with Thekla's commitment to the faith and that she seems to be a capable teacher."

"This is good news." I sighed wondering how long Thekla's adventure with this teacher and a new faith would last.

Lectra raised an eyebrow in question. "You seem uneasy."

"Thekla has had little experience alone in the world and she's traveling with a man I don't know. While I'm not her mother, I am concerned that she may unknowingly encounter difficulties because of her naivete."

Lectra tilted her head to the side while she thought about my comments. "Your concerns for Thekla's welfare are understandable. We know that she has received the blessing of the Holy Spirit because She brought the storm that released Thekla from the fire. As long as you are receptive to Her direction, you will always be supported in whatever circumstances you encounter. I am confident that wherever Thekla goes and whatever she encounters the Spirit will be with her."

I looked down at my hands to avoid looking at Lectra. I knew she meant well, but her comments were not very comforting.

"Paul is committed to a life of celibacy because he feels that physical involvement will deter him from sharing the teachings of Jesus Christ. In addition, he is not a physically attractive man being short, partially bald with a very large hooked nose and bowed legs." I couldn't help but laugh with her before she continued, "His appearance is an advantage because he doesn't attract women for his looks and once he speaks, a change comes over him that makes you want to hear every word. Thekla will be safe as she travels with him, but being respectful of the ways of the Spirit, he will not intervene on her behalf in case a situation develops that can lead to furthering people's understanding of Jesus' teachings."

I leaned toward Lectra. "What faith you have in these teachings! So much of what I see in your house and hear you say turns the world I've known upside down. To be totally reliant on the will of a spirit seems unwise, at best. I look at your home and see a range of people living and working together as if they were related and yet the situation goes beyond anything I understand about a family household and friendship." I was so confused that I couldn't find the best way to describe how I felt about all that she said. At a loss for words, I just stopped talking.

Lectra looked at me with an expression of complete confidence and said, "This way of life is supported by a faith in the Unknown God and his son Jesus Christ. The first time Onesphorus told me about Paul, I was shocked at the change in his attitude. My concerns were so strong that I decided I had to meet Paul too. I wasn't swayed the first time I heard him speak, but on reflection about his teachings, I began to understand and yearned to know more. We've made it a point to learn as much as we could about the life of love and forgiveness. Much to everyone's surprise, I was the one to propose that we open our villa to other believers and offer a refuge for Paul whenever he comes to Iconium."

I knew that I should feel comforted, but anxiety still gnawed at me. My confusion about these new beliefs worked to heighten my worry about Thekla. When food was served, they prayed to the Unknown God giving thanks for what they had received and ended with a request that Paul and Thekla be blessed on their journey and in their work.

After we finished eating, I said good-bye to Lectra and walked home thinking about all that I had seen and heard. I never believed in gods or goddesses. As a slave, I had no involvement with the temples. When I became a hetaera, I was forbidden access to all temples, except

Aphrodite's. My credo has been to live each day in the best way I can without causing harm to another person or animal. My experiences as a slave had developed a deep sense of compassion in me for any helpless being. I had no thought of an existence beyond this life and believed that there was nothing more for me after I died. Comments about the risen Jesus puzzled me.

It was late in the afternoon when I got home. I stood for moment in the street and compared it with the two huge villas I'd just seen. My tiny house brought a smile to me face. It was perfect for me. I opened the front door, pulled off my palla, and went directly to the garden where I could relax and read Thekla's letter.

Dearest Friend Daphne,

The walk to Lystra has been very interesting because Paul talks to everyone we encounter. This gives me the opportunity to learn more as he speaks with them. Many people are anxious to find something to hold on to that is stronger than the gods and goddesses that are so human in their demands and petty rivalries. It reassures them to hear about a God that cares about them and doesn't demand exorbitant offerings.

By the time we reached Lystra, one of our fellow travelers invited us to stay in his villa and share the teachings with his family. When we have finished our work here, we will go to Antioch where Paul has met with people before. That will be my next opportunity to send a message to you.

Perhaps you've been able to get to know Onesiphorus's household. I hope you will learn from them about the work Paul and I do.

May you come to know Jesus's love.

Thekla

I put down the letter and sighed. Being with Lectra and her household had been a pleasant experience, but it hadn't reassured me about Thekla's obsession with the new teachings. Who was this Jesus and what did he know about love? Thekla was young and inexperienced.

Was she infatuated with this silk-tongued Paul? I was concerned about her safety, but I was just a friend, not her mother. Questions roiled inside me until I had a headache.

It all seemed so foreign to the Roman way of life, whose laws and customs were not easy for women. This path Thekla was following didn't seem to be one that would offer any kind of secure future.

Alexander of Syria

Letters from Thekla came as she was able to take time from her traveling and teaching, but I wanted to know so much more. The two I had received were not enough to satisfy me. When Lectra sent a message that she wanted to visit me again, I wasn't sure what to think. Perhaps she wanted to follow up on my reaction to seeing her household. Only as an afterthought did it occur to me that she might have news of Thekla.

Lectra's arrival at my villa in midmorning surprised me because I had assumed that she would send one of her sons with a letter from Thekla. As soon as I saw her face, I knew that she brought distressing news. We walked into the courtyard garden where I had refreshments waiting for us.

After we were seated, she took my hand and spoke in a soft voice. "Daphne, we've received some disturbing news from Paul, and I have another letter for you from Thekla. I am troubled by what he has shared with us and decided to come to you rather than discuss everything in our active household."

The knot that had formed in my stomach when I first saw her at the door now tightened further. I found myself holding my breath.

"Paul said that as they approached Antioch of Pisidia, a man called Alexander confronted him, wanting to buy Thekla. It was apparent from his manner and attire that he was of considerable standing in Antioch. Paul brushed his demand aside, saying that she was not his to sell."

I recalled encountering officials like this man when I was a slave. One man wanted my owner to sell me to him, but he refused. I imagined Alexander's condescending manner toward a woman alone, believing that she was his for the taking. Fortunately, I'd never had direct involvement with such men. But, for Thekla, an inexperienced young woman, she would have been easy prey for him.

Lectra continued, "Suddenly, Alexander grabbed Thekla and assaulted her. She fought hard against him and a crowd gathered to watch them. When he couldn't get control of her, he ordered the guards to seize Thekla and had her taken to the governor's tribunal. Because she humiliated him and showed no respect for his office as city councilor, Alexander demanded that she be thrown to the animals and killed."

As Lectra talked, I grew lightheaded and leaned against the couch. She poured a cup of wine for me to sip. Tears welled in my eyes as I thought about Thekla being attacked by animals. I could hardly keep my composure. Finally, I gestured for Lectra to continue.

"The governor tried to intervene, suggesting other punishments for her, but Alexander wouldn't change his demands. With no other option, the governor finally declared that she would fight the beasts. Queen Tryphaina, a widow and a relative of the emperor offered to take care of Thekla until everything was ready."

I was speechless as tears streamed over my cheeks. Lectra paused and fixed herself a cup of wine. As my tears subsided, she refilled my cup and passed it to me. We sat in silence for several minutes.

Suddenly Lectra burst out, "Paul's actions bother me a lot sometimes. Once Thekla was under the Queen's care, he left Antioch for Myra."

I took her hand and held it gently. "Didn't Paul do the same thing regarding Thekla in Iconium? He didn't try to find out what happened, but stayed with your family in the cave."

"In his defense, he had no choice then since he was taken directly from the court to be flogged and then physically thrown out of the city. If Onesiphorus hadn't been prepared to take him and care for his wounds, I'm not sure what would have happened to him. I know that he didn't forget Thekla because he led our prayers for her until she arrived."

I listened, but I was incensed by Paul's disregard for Thekla's well-being. "I have never met Paul and I don't understand your way of faith. It is very hard for me to accept how he treats Thekla."

The silence between us lengthened, until finally Lectra spoke.

"For as long as I have been a Christian, I have found that no one interferes with events as they unfold." Lectra thought carefully as she talked. "We believe that the work of the Holy Spirit is beyond our capacity to understand and that our intervention could prevent further benefit for all people. The example comes from when Jesus was crucified in Jerusalem on trumped up charges with no evidence. He died as an example for us to love others to the extent that we are willing to give our lives for each other and to show us that death is not to be feared."

My voice was stern as I said, "It sounds like you expect some good to come from Thekla's death."

"I . . . think so, but who knows what is possible with the Holy Spirit." Tilting her head to the side as she often did as she was thinking, Lectra said, "I would not have imagined that Thekla could have escaped the fire, but she did. Now, as she is to face wild animals, I don't know what might happen, but I will pray that her life fulfills the purpose of the Holy Spirit as she has committed herself to this faith and way of life." Lectra's convictions strengthened her voice.

"Don't you ever doubt the practice of allowing things to unfold?" I asked in disbelief.

She shook her head. "My experience has been that when things are meant to be different, an alternative for us to follow presents itself. It's when we've struggled against things we don't like, when no other way is possible that the greatest sadness assaults us. It's not only the distress that follows, but also the sense of failure for not trusting the Holy Spirit."

Her comments troubled me, but she was a guest in my house and I didn't want to argue with her. I valued her willingness to bring Thekla's letters to me personally when she could just as easily have sent one of her sons. It seemed to me that these new believers dealt with issues with passive resignation rather than confronting the issue and working toward a fair solution or safe outcome. And this approach to providing for Thekla's safety was deeply disturbing.

Lectra handed me a thick scroll and asked, "Would you like me to stay with you while you read it? I don't need to know what it says, but if you'd like me to keep you company for a while, I'd be glad to."

For some reason, I found Lectra's presence comforting. "Thank you. Please stay a little longer." I looked at the scroll in my lap. It was of much finer quality than anything Thekla had sent before and was very thick.

Dearest Daphne,

Perhaps news of my arrest in Antioch has reached you before this letter. If not, talk with Onesiphorus or his wife, Lectra as I'm sure that Paul has communicated with them about it.

The journey from Lystra to Antioch was uneventful, but trouble started as we approached the edge of the city where a city councilor decided that he must possess me. When Paul did not sell me to Alexander, the man assaulted me and tried to drag me into a dark alley to satisfy his lust. Having vowed that I would remain celibate, dedicated to living according to Jesus's teachings, I fought to save my virginity. While he lost his crown and his mantle of office was torn as we fought, he became the laughingstock of the crowd which had gathered around us. They ridiculed him for being unable to subdue a mere woman. Humiliated, he called for soldiers to take me before the governor's tribunal.

Alexander demanded that I be sent to the arena where the wild animals would be released. The governor offered several other punishments, but the proud fool was not swayed and continued to insist that the beasts tear me apart.

He said that he would provide some of them himself. The governor was left with no alternative.

Finally, I had a chance to speak and I asked for more secure arrangements while I was being held. I knew that if I were sent to prison, Alexander would bribe the guards to allow him access to me. Having expressed my concerns, Queen Tryphaina asked that I be given to her until the date of my punishment.

Queen Tryphaina was widowed a few years ago and more recently lost her only daughter, Falconilla. She took me to her home and treated me as if I were her daughter giving me Falconilla's clothes to wear and her rooms for my use as long as I remained in her care.

I know that they are preparing the amphitheater and collecting more fierce animals for the people's entertainment. One day soon, someone will take me to face my punishment.

Daphne, I trust fully in the God of Jesus and accept all of his teachings. The Holy Spirit will be with me each step of the way so I have no fear of what lies ahead. I grieve for you because you are the one closest to me and I love you. I wish that I could protect you from this knowledge now. My hope is that you will grow in understanding of this faith and remain close to Lectra and Onesiphorus. Forgive me for causing you more pain. Know that I love you and treasure your friendship now and always,

Thekla.

I must ask you for help with one last task. You will have discovered another letter wrapped with this one. Please give it to Gaius for him to execute my will.

The letter slid off my lap as hot tears flowed over my face. Sobbing, I felt Lectra pull me into her arms and hold me as if I were a child needing to be comforted. No one had held me with such tenderness for years. I wept without restraint. She asked no questions, but stayed by my side until I was calm, then summoned my maid to request water so that I could wash my face.

I don't remember when Lectra left because my maid saw her out while I stayed alone in the garden. Numbness crept over me. I had no desire to move. When darkness fell, my maid lit the oil lamps and asked if I would come inside. I wanted nothing, nothing except for Thekla to be safe with me again.

I woke the following morning in my bedroom without remembering leaving the garden. Sheets were tangled around my legs as if I'd been in a fierce struggle. A feeling of dread clung to me and for a moment, I forgot what had happened, but as soon as I swung my legs off the couch, I saw Thekla's letter on the floor. Finally, I got up and dressed, knowing that, for Thekla's sake, I needed to move. The first task would be to contact Gaius.

I was nearly oblivious to the beautiful day as the cloud of sadness over Thekla's fate darkened everything I tried to do. In the early afternoon, I gave up my usual chores and waited for Gaius in the living room. The bright colors I normally enjoyed now annoyed me. Life seemed muted. How could these colors remain so vibrant when I was consumed with sorrow for Thekla?

Gauis's voice broke the silence as he greeted my maid and she showed him into the room. He paused as soon as he saw me, shocked at my appearance. I knew that my eyes were red and swollen. I'd taken no care with cosmeta or to do more with my hair than comb it.

He dispensed with normal greetings and asked, "What happened?"

I moistened my lips and in a flat tone of voice said, "Thekla is to be executed, or perhaps she has already been torn apart by the wild beasts."

He reached for my hand and held it. "If you can, tell me what has happened to her."

I thought that I had exhausted my supply of tears, but as I began to talk, they returned again. He listened carefully and never interrupted. When I finished, I gave him the letter she had written to him.

He searched my face before asking, "May I read it here in case I need your advice?"

I nodded and poured wine for each of us as he began to read. He went over it twice and then handed it to me to read.

Honorable Gaius,

This letter is to serve as my will. There is no need to wait before proceeding with these bequests as I believe that I will not belong to this world very much longer. Daphne will tell you all that has happened in Antioch. My accuser is quite a powerful man; even the governor could not sway him.

Please arrange the necessary documents so that all my servants at the country estate will be free. In addition, divide the property itself and my wealth equally among them: Pallas, Acca and our caretaker's family. With these resources, they are free to remain at the estate and live together or return to their homes. Whatever Pallas and Acca choose to do, I want my father's caretaker and his family to be able to remain at the estate as owners of their house and the acres that will become their share.

While this sounds a bit complicated, I don't want any of them to be forced out, except as they choose. If Pallas and Acca decide to build dwellings for themselves on the land, there is adequate acreage for them to do so and have money left over to live on for a short period of time. (Note that in all instances, Acca's share is to be equal to that of the men.) If Pallas and Acca decide to return to their homelands, the land they would receive reverts to the caretaker.

My deep desire is that they all be free to pursue the lives of their own choosing.

I wish that I could tell you face to face how much your support has meant to me. My father treasured you as his dearest and most trusted friend and I, too, hold you in that regard.

May love, peace and happiness be yours.

Thekla

I passed the letter back to Gaius. For some reason, reading her will eased some of my distress. Her thoughtfulness for the others who depended on her made me proud of her, that even as she waited for her brutal execution, she continued to care for them. I had no idea that she had such a deep capacity to care for others. Whether this ability was an aspect of her I had never seen or one that developed from her new faith, I didn't know. Surely her trust in this new God was profound to enable her to compose the letters and speak no ill of Paul for abandoning her. I was furious with him and at the same time very grateful for Queen Tryphaina's involvement.

Gaius glanced at the letter and then rewound the scroll. "I will follow her directions, but for as long as her servants and estate are safe, I feel no urgency to proceed."

"If I could make a suggestion, Gaius, please start the process for freeing her servants."

He looked at me with such a puzzled expression that I thought I should explain.

"I grew up not far from here in the village of Daphne. My parents were unaware of regional fighting until soldiers burst into our villa. My father was killed and my mother probably raped. I was taken as a slave. In Greece, a kind man bought me to serve in his household. When he died unexpectedly, he had arranged for all his slaves to be freed. Each one was given money to be able to leave the city, return to their home or pursue some other goal. Thekla knew my background and it may have prompted her to write this will."

Gaius's face turned pink. "I had no idea, Daphne."

"There is no reason for people to know, but it seemed appropriate to tell you so that you could understand Thekla's request and my support of her in this." For the first time since Lectra's visit the day before, I was able to smile sincerely.

"Thank you for explaining everything to me. I'm glad that I read the letter while I was still with you." He scowled in thought. "My first duty is to Thekla. I need to verify her death; I will not be hasty in executing her will in case there is some last minute reprieve. If she survives, she will need both her home and her money. At that point, if she still wants to release her servants, we can finalize their papers."

We both relaxed against the cushions breathing easily for the first time since he had arrived. I poured wine for us and passed him his cup. We drank as if we'd gotten very thirsty from hard work.

I refilled my empty cup and offered more to him. "May I make a request of you?"

"Of course." Gaius gave me his full attention.

"If you find out that Thekla has survived. Please let me know. Especially, if she needs physical care of her wounds. I would bring her here and care for her." Tears welled in my eyes, but they did not spill over.

"I will keep you up to date on any information I receive about her and my progress with her requests."

Silence grew between us, disrupted only by birdsong. He set his empty cup on the table and wound the scroll to tuck inside a concealed pouch. We stood up together and I walked him to the door.

Paraded in Antioch

In four days, Gaius returned to my villa with news about Thekla. From the moment I received his message until he was seated in my living room, I paced in the courtyard and walked through every room to calm myself. When I heard someone at the door, I was the first to get there and let him in. He was smiling and I knew that Thekla was alive.

Before we could seat ourselves in the courtyard, he burst with the news. "Thekla is alive and well!"

I was stunned. "How is this possible?" Without thinking I hugged him as if he were a brother. "Tell me everything." I poured wine for us and spilled some from my cup at my corner altar in gratitude to Thekla's Unknown God.

"I couldn't be comfortable in Iconium without knowing all of the details of Thekla's situation. I felt compelled to get there and act on her behalf, if at all possible. I got to Antioch just as they were closing the gate of the amphitheater. The only place left was standing room in the front row next to the moat. Behind me in the reserved, upper seats was the governor and beside him Queen Tryphaina. I wanted to get close to him in case there was an opportunity to intervene on her behalf, but the jostling crowd was packed so tightly I was fortunate to remain on my feet.

"I asked those around me to explain what was going on. They said that Alexander had delivered the beasts to the stalls of the amphitheater the day before. He'd made a big spectacle of it by parading Thekla, naked astride his lioness ahead of all the other animals. People lined the streets to see the amazing sight. Many jeered at Alexander because, from the time of her arrest, rumors had run wild about how he had assaulted her. Now the crowd filled the amphitheater to capacity. A deafening roar when Thekla was brought in stopped further discussion.

"The first lioness was released on the opposite side of the amphitheater. It was a huge beast and the speed with which she ran across the arena startled me so that I moved back into the crowd. She charged directly toward Thekla, who remained very calm and even seemed to open her arms to the animal as it approached. Just when I expected it to attack, incredibly it suddenly knelt at Thekla's feet! Some say it was the lioness that she had ridden the day before.

"Then another lion with a massive dark mane entered charging toward Thekla, but the lioness killed him before he could get close to her. As bears and other wild cats were unleashed, the lioness killed them all. Finally, she died from her wounds at Thekla's feet. Thekla bent down, stroked its fur, and seemed to talk to it as it took its last breath. An atmosphere of sadness descended on everyone in the amphitheater. The crowd was almost silent so I turned when I heard a man's loud angry voice. Alexander gestured wildly and insisted to the governor that Thekla should be tied to his bulls for them to tear her apart. I knew that the crowd could not hear Alexander's demands so I was surprised to hear the audience moan. I whipped around scanning the ground and saw that as Thekla was waiting, she had jumped into the inner moat of wild seals. I thought this was her attempt to avoid Alexander's bulls. The crowd roared its approval when she surfaced. I was close enough to see her radiant face and hear her shouting praise to the Unknown God. The seals that should have attacked her seemed stunned by her actions."

Gaius swallowed some wine and continued. "Two huge bulls were harnessed and brought inside where Thekla was lashed between them. The glow that I first saw when she came out of the water made her face shine even as they were tying her in place. The bulls didn't move, but stood docile as cows. So, Alexander took fire and placed it beneath them to force them to run, but the flames burnt the ropes holding Thekla and she slid to the ground unharmed. At this point, the governor stood up and released her from further attacks and punishment.

"I was pleasantly surprised by his actions. Later I found out that when the flames were set under the bulls, Queen Tryphaina fainted. They said that because she is a relative of Caesar, the governor stopped the event so that she could be tended to. Also in deference to the queen who had taken care of Thekla, I believe he gave her clemency to reduce the risk of any further harm to Tryphaina and the possibility of reprimand from the emperor."

Tears of joy covered my face and I couldn't stop smiling.

Gaius smiled too and said, "That evening, I went to Queen Tryphaina's villa and asked to speak to Thekla. She was happy to see me and asked me to visit you as soon as I returned to Iconium so that you would know she's is alive and unharmed. She insists that I proceed with the directions she wrote in her letter to me. I tried to convince her to save something for her own use, but she refused, saying that the Holy Spirit had provided for her so far and she counted on Her to stay near regardless of what the future brings. I felt uneasy about fulfilling her directives, but there was nothing I could say to change her mind." Gaius shook his head and lifted the cup to his lips for a long drink.

"When Queen Tryphaina joined us, she asked me to formalize her adoption of Thekla. We completed the required documentation and registered Thekla as her daughter the following day. This unexpected development relieved my concerns about Thekla's financial security, but I feel as though I should have done something more for her."

My immediate, involuntary reaction to this news of Thekla's adoption was a sharp stab of jealousy. I had cared for her all through her childhood and helped her elude her mother after the judgement in Iconium. For a fleeting moment, it felt as if she had abandoned our friendship. My expression must have revealed some of my thoughts because Gaius spoke before I could react.

"The Queen is hopeful that as her daughter, Thekla will have more protection if she is accused of any wrongdoing in the future. In addition, at the queen's death, Thekla is her sole beneficiary. At this point, Thekla again asked me to proceed with the instructions she had written in her will so that her servants would be free and have the resources of the estate if they choose."

"So her home will be in Antioch now." I looked at the fish swimming in the pool so that I didn't have to see Gaius's face when he replied.

"Thekla told me that she intends to follow Paul to Myra, but she will cut her hair and dress as a young man. The queen has accepted the teachings of Jesus and supports Thekla's decision. She will see to it that Thekla has the right clothing and funds to help her find Paul."

I shook my head in anger and disbelief. "How can she still follow this man?" I knew there were no answers for this question, except to hear from Thekla herself. My emotions were reeling from all that Gaius had said and I felt relief as he left. Alone I could work through the events he described in Antioch and explore my own reactions. Then I would be able to move forward and find whatever new way needed to be established with Thekla.

A Royal Summons

T wo weeks passed without any news of or from Thekla. I assumed that she must have gone to Myra. Obsessed with jealousy of the queen, I wondered whether Thekla might write to her new adopted mother rather than maintain contact with me. She had given away most of her possessions around Iconium and might not have a need to . . . I shook my head vigorously and tried to get rid of these thoughts that demeaned both Thekla and me. She was not one to cast people off like old clothes.

I immersed myself in work to complete the overdue repairs to the villa. While there was not a lot of damage from the storm that saved Thekla's life, I hadn't taken the time to examine the villa carefully or hire workmen. I was walking around the exterior walls when a messenger delivered a scroll sealed with wax bearing a royal imprint. I knew no royal personage so this message could not bring any good news. Although curious, I was in no hurry to read it. First, I finished the inventory of repairs that needed to be made and finalized arrangements for them so that they could begin working in the morning.

A scent of roses lingered in the air as I sat in the garden. Under normal circumstances, I would have leaned back and breathed deeply, but I couldn't ignore the letter in my lap. I examined the scroll. The vellum was very high quality as would be expected for communication from a royal office. I studied the wax seal on the scroll before breaking it and reading the letter.

Greetings to you, Daphne,

Since we have never met, I am taking the bold move to contact you directly. Perhaps you have already heard the news about Thekla's arrest and punishment in Antioch. The Iconium magistrate Gaius visited me after the events in the theater. He was very helpful to both me and Thekla. Before he returned to Iconium, he suggested that I get to know you because you are a close friend of Thekla.

While I am the one who gave her protection and support when she needed it here, there is no doubt that she loves you dearly. She talked about you often while she was with me and longed to be able to see you herself. It saddened her to know that you would hear about her experiences in Antioch from someone else.

There was a time when I loved to travel and see new cities, but that is no longer possible for me. Consequently, I invite you to my home here.

We share a common bond in our concern for Thekla's well-being. Perhaps there is a way that, working together, we can find other opportunities for supporting her and her work.

I look forward to meeting you soon.

Queen Tryphaina

A sense of warmth from the friendship I bore Thekla filled me as I read the queen's letter. I used the corner of my palla to wipe away a tear. Our relationship may not have been broken as I feared. But the fact that Queen Tryphaina had adopted her still left me uneasy.

I reread the scroll. Her message was short and direct rather than filled with the more effusive phrases I thought were customary in correspondence from royalty. The way she wrote made me think more of her. That she had helped Thekla and had met Gaius made me curious to meet her.

I had already scheduled minor repairs to be done on the outside walls of my villa. This meant that, although there was nothing pressing on my calendar, I could not leave until the work was finished, in about two weeks. My reply to the queen was as courteous and brief as hers to me, but at least she would know when to expect me.

I chose to travel by litter because I was no longer accustomed to walking long distances. As soon as we left Iconium, I opened the curtains to watch as I passed the countryside. How I loved the rolling hills of the fertile farms. Except for a few brown fields lying fallow, the scene was filled with various patches in green hues according to the type of grain and stage of its growth. With my eyes closed, I could smell the robust scent of the grasses.

The first settlement we passed through was Daphne, the village for which I had been named. We stopped there for a break and I walked around half hoping, half dreading that I would recognize something or someone from my childhood long ago. When I took my seat once more in the litter it was with mixed feelings of relief that nothing had appeared familiar.

Two days later, I arrived in Antioch. As we passed through the crowded streets, I watched the people and wondered about the demanding, pompous Alexander who had assaulted Thekla. How could this man, known to be a Syrian, wield such power in a foreign city? It could not be political connections, but must have been the way he disbursed his excessive wealth.

The queen's residence was located on the far side of Antioch from where I'd entered. My transit through the center square made it possible to see much of the city including glimpses of the huge market and the amphitheater.

Queen Tryphaina's villa was set back from the street with a gated entrance manned by two guards. As soon as they heard my name, they allowed my litter to enter. Trees lined the short path to the steps in front of the columned entrance where the queen appeared with two attendants.

She was much smaller than I had imagined. Elegantly attired with a narrow gold band fastened to her hair as a crown, she held out both hands to welcome me. When I took her hands in mine, they felt cool and very fragile. Her artfully styled brown hair was threaded with white strands. The extreme pallor of her skin was natural, not due to cosmeta, and I wondered about her health.

Queen Tryphaina linked her arm in mine and led me inside to the rooms she had prepared for my use while I was visiting. The accommodations were stunning and more spacious than my entire house. The color scheme blended blues with purple and turquoise, a combination that I enjoyed very much.

"Daphne, when you are settled and rested, a servant will guide you to my garden for refreshments."

"Queen Tryphaina, thank you for your hospitality. I will join you in a little while." As I spoke, she shook her head.

"Please call me Tryphaina. I am a widow and no longer serve as a queen. It is a title that has its use, but among friends, there is no need for it."

I couldn't believe my ears. We had just met and the Queen was calling me a friend. My social circle as a hetaera was very limited by society. I was more accustomed to being shunned than received warmly as a friend. It drew me to her with a desire to know her much better.

Once I had washed and unpacked a few things, I asked the maid to guide me to where Tryphaina was waiting. She sat in a secluded corner of a large courtyard with a noisy fountain in the middle. It made a pleasant, soothing sound and I heard a few birds in the shrubs. Tryphaina was stretched out on a lounge supported with several pillows. I was relieved to note that she had more color in her face now than when I had arrived.

"Daphne, thank you very much for coming. At this point in my life, I enjoy each day, but don't go out very often. I normally avoid events in the amphitheater, but with Thekla, I had to be there. You must have some questions about all that happened to her while she was in Antioch. Perhaps I can offer some answers."

The only question I wanted to ask Tryphaina, but wouldn't, was:

Why did you adopt Thekla? I assumed that over the course of my visit, I could figure out the answer for myself.

The queen chuckled softly when I didn't respond. "I didn't intend to put you on the spot," she said. "Perhaps it will help if I tell you a bit about myself. And how I met Thekla."

I grinned and said, "Thank you."

"The king and I governed a small area east of Galatia subsequent to appointment by the emperor who was a cousin to both of us from different branches of the family. At that time, he needed people he could trust to rule over outlying areas of the empire. When my husband died, I had no desire to take over the responsibility of governing and moved to Antioch. My daughter Falconilla was betrothed to an officer in the emperor's troops serving in Gaul and she decided to live with me until his return. We had lived here six years when she became seriously ill."

Tears welled in Tryphaina's eyes and she reached for a cup of wine before continuing. "When Falconilla died a year ago, I considered returning to Rome where I still had some family. But I couldn't face leaving the land that held my husband and daughter, so I never left." She paused as a look of remembrance passed across her face.

"I'm very sorry for your losses." It seemed a trite thing to say when I heard myself. I was grateful that she had taken the initiative to talk about her life, but regretted the sadness that it caused. "Tell me how you met Thekla."

A warm smile brightened her expression. "As a courtesy, the governor invites me to sit with him whenever he holds court. We often chat as he waits for people to come before him. This particular day, the city councilor, Alexander demanded that his complaint be heard ahead of others. That man is always agitating about something. Although he is from Syria, he has given so much financial support to the city for various improvements that he can't be dismissed easily. His fury with Thekla was obvious before he described his complaint.

She had not only refused his advances, but fought so vigorously that his mantle was torn and his crown dirty from falling on the ground. I truly admired her for fighting him." A flash of annoyance erased her smile. "I was appalled when Alexander insisted that she be thrown to the beasts as punishment. No matter what alternative sentence, the governor suggested, Alexander would not change his mind. He wanted her destroyed publically as if that would ease his humiliation by a young woman. When I glanced at Thekla, she stood calmly and showed no hint of fear until she was to be taken to the prison. Then, she asked for more secure confinement and I offered to take her. I knew that Alexander would find a way to satisfy himself with her unless she was with me."

I sighed without intending to. "Thank you for all you've done for Thekla. I've been anxious for her well-being since she left Iconium."

Tryphaina seemed to relax and we sat in comfortable silence enjoying the garden with the music of the water splashing in the fountain. It was a beautiful courtyard with varieties of plants and flowers I didn't recognize. Birdsong filled the air and I felt at peace for the first time since Thekla turned up at my villa cut and bruised. The shadows lengthened and the air cooled. Tryphaina looked tired as she rubbed her hands over her arms warming herself from a chill.

"Let's talk later this evening," I suggested.

"I'm afraid that I tire easily these days and there is so much more that I want to share with you. After dinner we'll both have more energy."

I slept well that night. It wasn't my own bed, but I sank into its softness and imagined I was sleeping in the clouds. I awoke refreshed and ready for whatever the day would bring. Tryphaina was sitting in the courtyard eating fruit and flatbread when I joined her.

Her smile was warm and genuine. "I'd forgotten how nice it is to talk with someone about difficult situations. It can be exhausting to

explain all of the background information. You are such a good lis-
tener, I feel that I can talk about all that has happened recently without
the need to go into great detail. Let me tell you about my daughter
before we return to Thekla."

I nodded my agreement.

"Falconilla died suddenly in her sleep. The previous day we had
gone to the market together and were planning a dinner party for the
following month. Our last conversation was full of laughter as we proposed guests to each other knowing full well the other did not care
for them. It had been a delightful day and evening. The shock that she
had died during the night was almost too much to bear. We had been
very close, not just mother and daughter, but best friends. Her loss
was very difficult to accept. I stayed secluded in the villa for a couple
months and refused to see anyone. Finally, the governor drew me
out by having me sit with him whenever he held court. Despite the
outcome of Thekla's trial, he is truly a kind man and tries to be fair in
the way he governs.

"When I brought Thekla home, I felt in some strange way as if I
already knew her and gave her my daughter's room and clothes. As we
got to know each other, I learned about her convictions and that the
teachings of Paul consumed her. He came to visit her before leaving
for Myra. They talked together for a long time and when he left, he
blessed us both."

That afternoon, Tryphaina called for her litter and took me to the
amphitheater. We went up to the reserved section and she pointed
out where Thekla had stood and explained how the animals were released. There was still a black spot in the sand where the ropes on the
bulls had burned. Tryphaina sat in the place where she had been that
day and patted the next place for me to take a seat.

Her eyes roamed the arena and then she began to talk. "Because
Thekla was so calm about being thrown to the wild animals, I found
that I could be calm too. We valued every hour without concern for

distant possibilities. When Alexander came with his lioness to have Thekla paraded through the streets, I tried to object, but there was no response from the governor. News of the spectacle had already spread like wildfire through the city. My desire to change the course of events was pointless. The next day, Alexander returned to take Thekla under guarded escort to the amphitheater, like a common criminal. The governor sent an escort for me, but I would not leave until after she had gone. In the amphitheater, I took my place here, next to the governor and his wife." She gestured with her hand, pointing to the gates and the moat before us.

As you can see, from this reserved section, there's an extensive view of all the gates where animals were released. The seals are clustered below us on the rocks in the inner moat just as they were that day."

She took a deep breath, then said, "Trumpets sounded, guards pushed the main gates just far enough for Thekla to enter the arena with only a narrow girdle tied around her waist. Suddenly the gate opposite her opened and the lioness charged across the sand at Thekla, but when she got within a few feet, she lifted her nose and sniffed the air. Then, the lioness laid down in front of Thekla. Within minutes another gate opened and a male lion charged them. The lioness stood up and tore him to shreds. It seemed that more animals were released as soon as the lioness dispatched them until there were no more beasts left. The lioness took her position in front of Thekla bleeding profusely from her wounds. The amazing beast looked up once and died."

"How incredible!" Although I'd already heard the story, Tryphaina spoke about it in such a way that I was mesmerized. I imagined the scene from Thekla's entry to the release of animals. A tear rolled down her cheek when she spoke of the lioness that died protecting Thekla.

She wiped her face and continued in an angry tone. "Alexander wasn't satisfied. He told the governor that he would tie her to his bulls and have her torn apart. He didn't give the governor a chance to answer, but left to see that the beasts were properly yoked. I didn't see Thekla jump into the moat with the seals. The reaction of the crowd was mixed with some sections cheering her and others booing with disappointment over the loss of another spectacle. Thekla ducked under the water and rose praising God, but not one seal came near her. I couldn't see her very well because I already felt lightheaded and needed to remain seated. By this time Alexander had brought his bulls inside."

She pointed at the moat below us. "With an angry shout, he ran to the moat, grabbed Thekla and heaved her out of the moat so that she could be tied between them. Once everything was secure, Alexander waved his cloak, but the animals stood still as if they were chewing cud. Then, he took a torch and lit the ropes to force the bulls to run from each other." Tryphaina smiled and continued with a twinkle in her eye. "At this point, I fainted and recall nothing until I woke on my couch at home. Later I found out that my collapse frightened the governor to the extent that he absolved Thekla of any wrong doing. I think he was afraid that I might die and he would have to explain the circumstances of my death to the emperor."

"What about Alexander? Did he try to do anything else?" I asked.

Grinning, Tryphaina shook her head. "The governor is so disgusted with him that he sent Alexander away on an errand out of the city and told the pompous fool not to return to his court for at least six months."

A New Gender

The following morning, the servant who had been caring for my needs told me that Tryphaina needed to rest and would see me later in the afternoon. She had asked the maid to take me to the market if I wanted to explore it. It was something I had hoped to do and suggested that we leave shortly. I rejected the use of the litter, but the maid insisted that we take one of the men with us.

The market was larger than the one in Iconium. One street perpendicular to the market square specialized with booths for scribes and all sorts of writing materials. The next one was lined on both sides with stalls of textiles from the coarsest materials to the sheerest silk. I stopped to look at many fabrics. Several of my curtains and cushions had been ruined in the storm that had saved Thekla's life from the fire. I hoped to find suitable fabric to replace the damaged items at home. It was tempting to buy some silk for a new toga and palla, but I was preoccupied with the household repairs and didn't want to focus on more clothes.

When we returned to the square, I stopped so suddenly that the maid walking behind me nearly knocked me over. The sight of a platform where slaves were being sold froze me to my core. My delight in exploring the market evaporated as the memory of being sold as a child assaulted me. I wanted to get out of there as fast a possible.

As soon as I had placed my purchases in the room I was using, I went to the courtyard and was surprised to find Tryphaina there.

"Daphne, I thought you would be in the market for hours. Is everything all right?"

The queen asked with concern.

"Our venture went well and I found some fabric to replace curtains at home." I paused and then said, "You've been so forthcoming with me about your life and all that has happened recently, I'll share some of my background with you."

Tryphaina nodded her encouragement.

"I was a child in the village of Daphne when troops came through fighting the Galatians. I was one of several children who were seized and sold as a slave in Athens. Seeing the slaves in the market today brought back horrific memories I hadn't thought about for a long time. I couldn't stay there while the bidding was going on. That's why I didn't explore more of the market. Perhaps another time."

Tryphaina's gaze was very intense and I wasn't sure what that meant.

"I beg your pardon if I have offended you," I said.

"Not at all, dear woman. I happened to recall something that Thekla said. We talked about her new way of life and she said that all people are created free and equal. The categories of slave, king, man and woman are artificial labels that we use, but have no meaning before the God of Love. That makes a lot of sense to me. I don't care who you have been. You are delightful to know."

I thought about telling her that I was known as a hetaera, but decided to let that drop unless she asked more questions.

She continued, "I've often wondered how my life might have been different if I hadn't been born into the emperor's family or, for that matter, born a woman. Leaving Rome to live here in the eastern Mediterranean region satisfied some of my longing to see other parts of the empire. I had no desire to govern alone, but it might have been nice to be free of the restrictions placed on women."

"I have led a very independent life and Thekla longed to do the same." I brushed fallen leaves off my toga as I organized my thoughts. "I believe that Thekla was quite startled when she discovered that her father had betrothed her to a business associate. She never mentioned it to me. Since Abrax rarely discussed his plans with me, I think he may not have told Thekla prior to his death. I can only guess that he planned to take his time introducing Thamyris to Thekla and offering them a chance to get to know each other. Perhaps he thought there would be months, if not years for them to get to establish a relationship before the wedding. Abrax's death was a shock to us all. A heavy burden fell on Thekla since her mother refused to be involved with his funeral rites." I frowned and tried to think about when she could have found out about the marriage contract. All I could remember was that every household was thrown into chaos as members sickened and died from the plague.

As Tryphaina waited for me to go on, she summoned a servant to being us refreshments. The wine soothed my dry throat and gave me a boost to continue.

"The idea of marriage shook Thekla because it was not the way she wanted to live. While I truly believe she is committed to these new beliefs, it also offers her the chance to break the contract and live on her own."

Tryphaina shook her head. "I don't know the details of your life or of Thekla's, but I think you've both paid a very heavy price to be free." A gentle smile returned to her face. "You've been very delicate with me, but let me put you at ease. Thekla told me that you are or have been a hetaera. She admires you tremendously and while she doesn't want to follow in your footsteps, she has learned a great deal from you beyond hair styles and cosmeta."

I laughed as I tried to imagine Thekla telling the queen about me. Tryphaina's smile deepened. As a result of our candor, a strong sense of friendship was growing between us.

The confidence that I lacked earlier surged.

"Tryphaina, Thekla wrote to me that you had adopted her. Tell me how that came about."

"Of course. I believe that you know the city magistrate from Iconium called Gaius." I nodded. "He got admission to the amphitheater just before they brought Thekla in to face the animals. After the event was over, he found his way here and asked to see her. She was delighted that he had come and they talked together for a couple hours, then asked me to join them. He had me witness the document he had prepared for her which freed her slaves and distributed all of her possessions to them. Prior to meeting Thekla, I had been trying to decide what to do with my estate. I knew that the emperor would claim it if I didn't make some arrangements before I died. As long as Falconilla was alive, I expected everything to go to her. When she was gone, I couldn't decide what to do. With Thekla and Gaius here, I knew immediately how the dilemma could be resolved. We had a short discussion and Gaius consented to draw up the documents for me to adopt Thekla and make her my heir."

"Thekla's last letter to me mentioned that you had adopted her." Any jealously I felt earlier was replaced with gratitude that Thekla had found such a friend.

"I had another motive which I didn't explain at the time although Thekla knows now. She told me briefly about the judgment against her in Iconium before arriving in Antioch. The dilemma she faced here was awful. My hope is that by adopting Thekla and making her the daughter of a Roman queen, she may have more security if someone tries to arrest her in the future. While I hope the need never arises, my actions also confer Roman citizenship to her which should help in any court throughout the empire." Tryphaina leaned against her cushions looking satisfied with what she'd been able to do for Thekla.

"You done something wonderful for Thekla and as her friend, I am grateful to you too. Thekla's father agonized over her future and tried to do everything he could to make sure that she would be well taken care of. He died before they could discuss plans for her future and the only option he could have imagined would have been a high society marriage. Now she can follow the life she has chosen."

Tryphaina nodded, then a smile spread across her face as her eyes twinkled. "We have been so serious in our discussions. Let's take a break from all that. Tell me about your visit to the market. I'm sorry that it was so brief. There's so much more to see and enjoy. Of all the stalls, the street with the textiles is my favorite. Time evaporates as I examine the wares. I never tire of looking at the textures and riotous colors. It's my favorite thing to do in the city. I'm glad that you found some fabric to take home."

"Would you like to see what I bought?" I asked and watched her eyes light up in anticipation. Tryphaina looked more rested than she had since my arrival.

She asked a servant to collect my purchases and bring them to us in the courtyard. Neither of us could resist touching the fabric as I explained how each would be used for curtains or to cover cushions for my courtyard. I unfolded them in the sunlight so that we could enjoy the quality of the color in the way the each one had been dyed. Tryphaina examined the weave of the fabrics to be used as curtains and held them up to see how light passed through. She sorted through the bundles again and frowned.

"Didn't you find something for a new toga and palla?"

I laughed. "I did think of that, but decided that these projects will keep me busy for now. Maybe next time."

Tryphaina's mood clouded suddenly. "The last time I went to the market was with Thekla. We were looking for something suitable for her to wear when she went to Myra to meet Paul. What began as a simple shopping trip for a modest toga and palla turned into a challenge to figure out how she could travel without drawing attention to herself. She is a stunningly beautiful young woman."

I nodded. "It was amazing to watch her develop into such a remarkable person. She was unaware of the impact her appearance had on others, especially men. When she left to search for Paul, I worried about her traveling alone. I had hoped that being with him might provide her with a measure of safety from predatory men, but that wasn't the case."

"Paul is neither a help nor a hindrance to the determination of other men who lust for her." Tryphaina paused in reflection before continuing, "The only solution I could come up with for her to travel alone and unmolested was for her to conceal her gender. At first, Thekla resisted the idea of traveling as a man. We discussed it many times, particularly for the compromising situation her appearance created for those with her. Finally, she agreed to the change. We found suitable taupe cloth and another length in dark brown for a cloak. When we got home and she dressed, I realized that her beauty was not concealed. That's when we decided to cut her hair. As the weight of its length fell off, the shorter locks revealed delightful curls that covered her head and framed her face. The short hair did alter her appearance to reveal a credible young man, if she altered her behavior to be more masculine. The last day that she was here, she wore the new clothes and went around the villa practicing gestures and walking like a man. Her comportment was convincing."

I refolded the bolts of cloth thinking about what Tryphaina had just told me. Although I understood the rationale that prompted the change, it was hard for me to imagine Thekla traveling disguised as a man. She was young enough to carry off the ruse, but how long would she need to maintain this charade? I wondered.

That afternoon a messenger arrived. Tryphaina asked me to join her after he left. She sat in the atrium with an unopened scroll in her lap and said, "This is from Thekla and it's addressed to both of us."

"How did she know I was here?"

Tryphaina blushed. "I sent a message to her in Myra so that she would know where we both were. She knew that I wouldn't travel, but I hadn't told her about your visit to Antioch. I hoped that she would write to us both while you were here in case there's more that we can do together to support her."

Tryphaina passed the scroll to me; I opened it and started to read, aloud.

Dearest Tryphaina and Daphne,

How happy I was to know that you have met each other and are together for several days. Seeing Antioch after my experiences there will give you, Daphne, a better understanding of what I was trying to explain in my previous letter.

Tryphaina, I am grateful to you for all that you have done and that you have opened your home to Daphne. How blessed I am to have both of you in my life.

Living as a man has brought me amazing freedom despite having to remember to act differently. It's not satisfying enough to want to continue indefinitely, but it has been helpful. Based on the conversations around me, hearing the way men talk about women, I was glad to avoid being the target of their attention as I walked to Myra.

It was easy to find Paul, but difficult for him to accept that the man before him was really me. Once we got over that hurdle, he was stunned that I had escaped the beasts without a scratch and praised God for my survival. When I told him how I jumped into the moat with the seals to baptize myself before death, he became very somber and said, "You have been correct in all that you have done. Truly you are a teacher, not only in your words, but also by example. Thekla, you have been blessed by the Spirit and are an apostle of the risen Jesus."

I was happy that he recognized my commitment to the faith and surprised that he applied the title to me that has been used for him, apostle (teacher). After this conversation, I worked with him speaking to smaller groups of people who could not get close enough to hear him. My joy with the work has surpassed my hopes. I know this is my life's work.

Paul and I have had long discussions about how best to proceed. Should I continue to travel with him dressed as a man? Should I revert to my normal appearance so that I can work more closely with women? Should we go different directions to reach more people with the message of love and forgiveness? We prayed for guidance and came to a mutual agreement that we need to go our separate ways to be more effective.

Although I can pass as a man very easily, I am uncomfortable concealing that I am a woman. If the truth were discovered, I am afraid it would invalidate all our teaching. Recent events have proved that it's not easy for me to travel alone as a woman which means that working in the manner of Paul is not feasible for me. He has suggested that I focus on one location to serve people. Without the need to travel, I can return to my normal dress and behavior. There is a town called Seleucia, not far from his home town of Tarsus. He thinks that it would be a good base for my work.

I have given careful thought to moving to this new place. First, I'll return to Antioch and spend some time with Tryphaina. When my appearance has returned to normal, with longer hair, I'll go to Iconium and stay with Daphne. There are several matters that need to be settled there before I relocate to Seleucia.

How I long to see you both. I have missed your friendship. When Paul is ready to leave Myra, I'll return to Antioch. I think we will leave in the next day or two and look forward to seeing you soon.

May the you be blessed with Jesus's love,
Thekla

When I looked up from the letter, Tryphaina's face was glowing. "I'll be so glad to see her again," she said.

"Yes, I am anxious to see her too. I can't decide whether I should wait for her here or hurry home to fix the curtains and cushions."

Tryphaina wore a pensive expression and said, "It has been much longer for you since the last time you saw Thekla. Why don't you wait for her so that we can all be together for a while? Then, you can return to Iconium and prepare for her visit."

Abiding Friendship

Thekla arrived the day after we received her letter. When I had last seen her she was recovering from cuts, bruises and general exhaustion. Even dressed as a man, I could see that she was strong and healthy. Her face was radiant with a ready smile. After greeting us, she went to Falconilla's rooms to bathe and change. Tryphaina and I waited for her in the courtyard as evening descended.

"I think she has found her purpose in life," Tryphaina said.

"I never imagined that she would become such a strong person and so daring, although I knew that she never wanted traditional married life." I had mixed feelings as I spoke because I wished for Thekla to have a safe future. Her experiences since she first heard Paul had brought great risks that made me deeply concerned for her future. I wondered what her life in Seleucia would be like and whether she would be safe there.

When Thekla joined us, dressed as a woman, she looked like the person I knew in Iconium. Although her hair was still very short, it was becoming.

She pulled a large cushion closer to where we were seated. "I am so glad to be out of those clothes. I like being a woman and there were times that I just wanted to stop the charade. Paul had so much difficulty adjusting to my appearance and behavior. At first he refused to believe it was me, but his distress was even deeper to discover that a woman was capable of dealing with challenges that face a man daily."

We all chuckled over Paul's limited understanding of women's strengths.

Then Thekla continued. "Our work together was so successful that he pushed his feelings to the side. I knew that we couldn't continue to travel together as two men. The strain would have been very hard for him and I had no desire to keep it up indefinitely. On the whole, the experience was good for both of us in different ways. He gained a new respect for the capacity of women that he didn't have before and my confidence was bolstered. After the clash with Alexander, I was afraid that I would need to be on guard all the time. Now I know that I can deal with almost any situation."

Truly, she had matured a great deal in recent months, and spoke with a confidence that she'd never shown before. Half joking, I said, "So you're going to keep a set of men's clothes, just in case?"

Thekla narrowed her eyes and thought. "I hadn't considered that, but it may be a good thing for me to do, at least until I'm settled."

There was a lapse in our conversation with each of us lost in our own thoughts, until, Tryphaina spoke up. "Have you considered your future plans in more detail?"

"If I'm going to relocate to Seleucia, I want to know more about the area and find a place to live. Even if I had a villa to move to now, I need basic household goods to make living there possible. I don't know whether to make those purchases in Seleucia or ship things from Antioch or Iconium."

I thought about my move from Greece to Iconium. I'd gotten rid of almost everything to make traveling easy. Once I found my villa in Iconium, I was able to fill it without any problem. "Why don't you select those things that you really like to take with you and buy the rest when you are in Seleucia?"

Thekla laughed. "With my belongings scattered at your home, the country villa and here, I'm not sure what I have."

"One thing is for sure, Thekla. You don't have to have everything immediately," Tryphaina said. "Find out where you will live and what you need. I have more furniture than I can use here. You can take whatever you want."

Thekla took Tryphaina's hand and squeezed it. "That's a generous offer, but I haven't given you the message from Paul."

"From Paul?" Tryphaina arched her eyebrows in surprise.

"He knows that you are committed to the new faith way because I've shared some of our discussions with him. He would like you to consider having a house church in Antioch for new believers. While there are many followers here, they have no place large enough to meet regularly and he has no place to use as his base whenever he comes to Antioch. His custom when I traveled with him was to find a modest inn where we could live and work. The length of our visit was determined by the money we had rather than the needs of the people we met." Thekla paused and shook her head at the thought. "I told him that I would tell you about his idea so that you can think about it. When he returns, he will come to see you first and find out what you think about it. "

Tryphaina rest her chin in her hand as she considered what Paul proposed. Finally, she gave a quick nod. "It's possible. I would be glad to be more active with the believers. This place is certainly large enough and there's a wing of the villa that he could use for his needs any time he's in Antioch."

I couldn't resist talking about the arrangement in Lectra's home. Tryphaina listened carefully as I described how they lived with a wide assortment of people.

"Well, I'll take things one step at a time," she said. "The villa is far larger than I need and I don't do formal entertaining anymore. The potential conflict could come as a consequence of having been queen. While I have few official duties, I don't want to create problems for believers. There are those in Antioch who feel that the new faith way is antisocial and on the verge of being illegal with its teachings about equality. Some are very worried about losing their servants if the beliefs are widely accepted."

Thekla nodded. "As I traveled back and forth to Myra, the men discussed their objections to the new faith. Many are afraid that women will refuse marriage. Others have heard of the house churches like Onesiphorus and Lectra have. They think such living arrangements are a threat to society. Although I thought a lot of their comments were bluster, they do raise valid issues that appear to be against the Roman law."

I looked directly at Thekla and said, "Defying Roman marriage laws is what gave Theokleia strength in her argument for your arrest in Iconium. As a hetaera, I was always aware of the risk as an independent woman. Most leading men support the institution for courtesans, but I doubt that they would allow us to remain celibate and live on our own. The new faith could be seen as disruptive to normal society, perhaps even a threat if it becomes popular."

Thekla listened carefully, then added, "Your points are well taken. My experiences teaching the new faith tell me that the Spirit will surmount any controversy, but resolution of the social uneasiness may take a long time, even years."

We continued to explore the objections to the new life style, particularly as it might affect Thekla's new work in Seleucia. None of us knew the region well, so many concerns were left unresolved.

When I awoke the next day, I was happy with the warm friendship that the three of us shared. I was also restless to get home and finish other repairs to my villa before Thekla returned. It took me most of the day to pack and arrange a litter for Iconium.

A few days after I returned home, I decided that I should visit Lectra and bring her up to date on Paul and Thekla. This time I walked in as if I were expected. As soon as Lectra saw me, she came to greet me with a warm embrace and kiss. Once we were seated and provided with refreshments, I began to tell her about my time in Antioch.

"So much has happened since I last saw you. Perhaps you remember that Thekla's letter mentioned Queen Tryphaina?" Lectra nodded.

"She sent me an invitation to visit her in Antioch and I just returned from her home two days ago. She took me to the amphitheater where Thekla faced the wild animals. Thekla's accuser was sent out of the city after the governor gave her clemency."

Lectra raised her eyebrows in surprise. "What a wonderful outcome to such a tragic situation. The Spirit has amazing ways that we cannot begin to understand."

I nodded and concealed my doubt about the action of the Spirit versus the governor's need to rid himself of a meddling, powerful person. I refocused on Thekla's journey. "Since Paul had already gone to Myra, Thekla decided to follow him. Paul acknowledged her as an apostle when he heard about how she survived the beasts. While they worked well together, it was difficult on both of them for Thekla to continue as if she were a man."

"It must have been quite strain for them both. Most actors are exhausted when they perform in a play. I can't imagine what it would have been like for them to maintain a constant pretense that Thekla was a man while working."

I smiled in a greement. "She returned to Antioch and Queen Tryphaina's villa just before I came back to Iconium."

"Isn't she going to teach anymore?" Lectra frowned.

"She and Paul discussed her role at length and they finally decided that they would continue to work, but independent of each other in different regions. He will keep up with his travels and probably have a permanent base in Antioch, if Queen Tryphaina and he can work out a plan for a house church there. By the way, I told Queen Tryphaina how your family have things organized here."

She nodded her approval. "But what about Thekla?"

"Paul has suggested that she develop a base in Seleucia where she can teach people without having to travel. Thekla will be able to dress normally as a woman and by remaining in one place will have less chance of problems with men who want her attention. Nothing has been settled yet. Thekla will stay with Queen Tryphaina until her hair is longer and then return to Iconium for a while before moving to Seleucia."

"I'm so glad to hear about the developments from you. We haven't heard from Paul for weeks. Sometimes he is so involved with his work that he has little time to write. The arrangements you describe for both Paul and Thekla sound good. I hope she will come see us when she is back."

"I'm sure she will. She said that there are several things she wants to finalize here before moving away. If she doesn't contact you first, I will make sure that you know when she's back." Having related all of my news, I leaned against the cushions.

Lectra offered fresh bread and olives. They were so delicious that we stopped talking for a while to savor them.

Finally Lectra said, "There have been some developments while you were away," she said. "Thamyris was in a freak accident driving his chariot. He was seriously injured and died from him wounds two days later. Being so young and with expectations that he would become a capable leader in Iconium, his death rocked the city. I've heard that Theokleia, for some reason, was particularly upset when he died. It was as if she had lost a family member. Since his parents died during the plague, she took over all of the arrangements for his cremation along with the appropriate offerings to the temples as if they were related."

I brushed crumbs off my toga and thought about Thamyris and Theokleia. Since Abrax had not told Thekla about the betrothal, she had never gotten to know Thamyris. I recognized his name, but I never knew him. "That is strange behavior for her because she made no arrangements when Abrax died. Thekla took care of everything when she was little more than a child."

Lectra adjusted the cushion behind her back and seemed distracted. Finally, she said, "Something seems odd about Theokleia's behavior. Before Thamyris's death she was trying, with his support, to get new laws passed in the city to apprehend fugitives. She sent her own guards to seize people she deemed as having thwarted the law. To my knowledge, she never succeeded in having anyone prosecuted a second time."

My hands turned cold as Lectra spoke thinking about Theokleia and her craftiness. I immediately thought of Gaius and decided that I would find out how far Theokleia had been able to proceed with her efforts to arrest and prosecute those who, in her opinion, escaped justice.

"I'm glad you told me about Theokleia's new campaign. When Thekla returned to Antioch, she mentioned that there were things she wanted to resolve here before moving to Seleucia. She will be staying with me so I'll be able to find out who she plans to visit."

When I left Lectra's home, I was preoccupied with what she had told me about Theokleia. By the time I reached my street, I was hurrying anxious to get a message to Gaius. Surely he would know whether Theokleia's new activities posed a threat to Thekla. It would be awful if she came back and walked into some trap set by her mother.

Planning for Seleucia

Gaius wasn't able to meet with me as soon as I'd hoped. It was midmorning, three days later, that he arrived at my villa. As soon as I heard his voice, my anxiety eased. We sat in the courtyard which was finally beginning to look normal again after the ravages of the storm. First he wanted news about Thekla's experience in Myra and her return to Antioch.

"She'll be returning to Iconium to resolve some issues. I don't know when or what her plans involve. Perhaps she'll be in touch with you directly. If not, I'll be sure to let you know what's happening."

His expression darkened when I said Thekla was returning to Iconium. "I wish she could go directly to Seleucia," he said.

"Queen Tryphaina, Thekla and I discussed her schedule before I came home and I haven't heard anything since then. She may turn up here unannounced. As soon as I hear from her, I'll let you know."

Gaius shook his head. "I need to see her before she visits anyone in the city."

"I'll keep you up to date with her plans." I didn't expect him to express concern about her movement around her hometown. "Why does her activity here bother you?"

He gave a half-laugh. "It isn't her behavior, but her mother's. Theokleia has not been successful in having laws passed for the immediate arrest of fugitives, but she has been hounding anyone she feels should be re-arrested and tried. As long as Thekla was away, I didn't worry about what Theokleia was doing, but I can see that she may try to have Thekla arrested and punished again."

"With all that Thekla has experienced since leaving Iconium, she won't be daunted by Theokleia's efforts."

Gaius reached over and held my hand for a moment. "Once we know Thekla's plans for her time in Iconium, we can figure out how to help her. As I said, Theokleia has not succeeded. The governor is getting tired of the way she harasses people by having her guards bring them to court. It is doubtful that she can do more than inconvenience Thekla, but I've never trusted Theokleia."

"Abrax was always on his guard because he knew that Theokleia would harm Thekla if she had a chance. He chose observant and faithful servants who would be alert for any mischief she might try."

We talked more about Thekla's work and her plans for Seleucia. By the time Gaius left, I felt more calm about Thekla's return, but knew that both he and I would have to be alert while she was in Iconium. Perhaps I should see Lectra again so that she could be available to help Thekla if she encountered problems. Lectra's villa was closest to Theokleia and she could respond more quickly if Thekla were detained there.

Three weeks had passed since I returned to Iconium from Antioch when I received a message from Tryphaina saying that Thekla had left and would be arriving at my villa within a few days. The repairs to the villa had been completed and the new curtains and cushions blended well with the older furnishings. The spare bedroom was ready for Thekla with the things she'd left behind carefully folded in storage baskets waiting for her.

Late in the afternoon, the servants called me to the door as Thekla stepped out of the litter and assorted packages were brought into the house. Her hair was a bit longer making it possible for her to pin a few curls in place. After directing the servants regarding her bundles and dismissing the litter, she came and hugged me. Despite my worries about her time in Iconium, I was thrilled to have her back. We talked until late into the evening and when I accompanied Thekla to her room, I was surprised to see how many parcels were stacked around the walls. She had a narrow path to the bed, but not much space to move.

She looked around and laughed. "After my time with Paul in Myra when I didn't have a change of clothes, it looks as if I've overcompensated by bringing too many things. Maybe you and I can sort through it all tomorrow."

For the first time in months, I woke refreshed without any nagging anxiety. I hummed to myself as I got dressed. Thekla was already seated in the courtyard eating fruit when I joined her.

"You look very pleased," she said.

"How could I be anything less? Having you back for a while has relieved me of all the concerns that I had as you traveled. What's your plan for today?"

Thekla thought for a moment. "I need to sort through everything here to figure out what I should keep and what things I may need for Seleucia. I know that Acca took my belongings to the country villa. I want to keep only those things I really like for my home in Seleucia. I've heard that it is a good sized coastal town with its own produce as well as imported goods. Anything I haven't got now, I should be able to get there easily."

"I've tried to learn more about the place," I said. "The town is upriver from the coast to deter raiders. You should be able to get good lemons, oranges and olives there. I think some of the citrus in our markets comes up from Seleucia. When we go to our market, you can talk to some of the vendors to find out more about local customs."

We were in no hurry to get started and continued our leisurely breakfast as Thekla talked about various people and places she'd seen on her travels. When we went to her room, she said, "The first thing I have to find is something from Tryphaina for you."

"But I don't need anything."

Thekla's eyes twinkled as she pulled open one basket after another finding what she wanted in the last one. She lifted out some fabric and reached for what was below. In her hands she held a piece of sky blue cloth with a second piece of darker blue fabric. "Here, this is for you from Tryphaina. She was sad that you didn't get back to the market to choose material for a toga and palla so she selected this for you."

The colors were perfect. I love all shades of blue. These were exquisitely dyed and so soft to touch. "I can't wait to wear them."

When we finally settled down to the task at hand, it was apparent that Thekla had a wide variety of cloth ranging from fine materials for clothes to coarser lengths for more practical needs. We stopped for lunch and then finished sorting and re-packing. When I looked at what we'd done, I realized that she had kept almost everything. I wondered what might be at the country villa and how many wagons she would need to go to Seleucia.

That evening Thekla asked if I had ever seen the country estate. As a hetaera, I had never been to the private homes of any of my clients and, following Abrax's requests had never accompanied her father to any function or property. He had always come to see me.

"Come with me tomorrow. We'll spend a couple days there. I never had a chance to talk to Acca and Pallas after my arrest here. I have missed them very much." She paused. "I want to walk around the estate once more before I move away."

I could think of no reason not to go with her and looked forward to the excursion. I would hire a wagon to take us and bring back whatever goods Thekla wanted for her new home.

Our arrival, late in the day, surprised Acca and Pallas who had chosen to live on the estate with the manager and his family. I thought that Acca would be about my age, but she appeared considerably younger. She couldn't have been very old when she started a caring for Thekla as an infant. She was taller than Thekla with a very pleasant manner, and I liked Acca instantly. Tears of joy covered her face as she embraced Thekla. Pallas held back observing them with a broad grin. His face was tanned from the sun with an old, deep scar on his left cheek. I knew that he had been a slave in other regions before Abrax found him to teach his daughter. The delight the three shared in seeing each other was contagious and lifted my spirits too.

Thekla introduced the manager, Telys, an older man whose married son, Hector lived with his parents and helped maintain the villa and orchards. With the money Thekla had given Telys, he and his son had begun an addition to their home. At present, Acca and Pallas shared the villa.

It was delightful to be included in everything as if I'd been part of Thekla's family in Iconium. While I thought Acca was still young, I noticed that her movements were slow. It made me wonder whether Theokliea had beaten her for helping Thekla see Paul in prison.

Acca assigned rooms to us giving Thekla the one she had used as a child. We had a chance to get settled and wash before the evening meal. Our meal was arranged in the large courtyard so that everyone could be with together.

Thekla offered a prayer, "Father - Mother of the cosmos thank you for the food you have given us for this day and for the understanding you have provided us for living in this world. Amen."

Everyone began to eat and as our hunger was sated, they asked Thekla about her travels.

"I had no idea what a surprising turn my life would take when I first started listening to Paul. What amazed me most was that once I was convinced of the authenticity of his teachings, I never felt afraid. As I waited to be taken to the fire in Iconium, I felt remarkably calm. During the storm, I became aware of a loving Presence that seemed to penetrate every fiber of my being."

Pallas raised a skeptical eyebrow and asked, "How did this radical awareness come to you?"

Thekla smiled tenderly as if he were a student. "Other followers of Jesus speak of similar insight once they commit themselves to living a life of love and forgiveness. I think my experience was triggered when I realized that Theokleia can't help being herself. But change is possible for her if she adopts the teachings from Jesus's life. This is true for everyone."

Acca eyed her critically and said, "I can't imagine standing still when wild animals are unleashed to tear me apart."

Thekla chuckled. "In some ways, that was the easy part. I knew what the animals were supposed to do. The amazing experience was how the lioness protected me. I felt sorry for her when I was forced to ride astride her the day before. I didn't do anything special with her, but she must have known that I meant her no harm. Surely regarding her in a loving way helped. The other beasts acted as I expected, but she defeated each one and then she died." She wiped a tear from her face.

Acca persisted with questions about Queen Tryphaina. Thekla told how Tryphaina sheltered her and eventually adopted her. We talked into the night reluctant to leave such good company, but the manager had early morning chores so his departure ended the festivities.

I stretched out on my bed listening to the sounds of the night birds and occasional hoot of an owl. This seemed to be a beautiful area, but too close to Iconium for Thekla's safety. The next thing I knew sunlight was streaming through the windows and I realized that I was hungry. Acca, Pallas and Thekla were seated together in a serious conversation as I joined them. When I hesitated, Thekla patted the cushions next to her for me to sit with them.

"Acca and Pallas were telling me about the recent visit of Theokleia's guards," Thekla explained giving me an inscrutable look.

I nodded and said, "Before you got home, I'd heard that Theokleia had become obsessed with capturing fugitives, but I thought her activities were mainly in Iconium."

Pallas raised his eyebrows as he said, "She sent her guards here to search for Thekla. When they didn't believe us, Telys and I showed them all around to prove that whatever Theokleia assumed about her daughter living in the country was untrue."

"They were not pleasant and made a mess in some of the rooms, especially Thekla's old room," Acca added.

"I got the impression that Theokleia may have promised them a bounty if they could bring her back to Iconium," Pallas said.

The conversation with Gaius came back to me and I shared it with them. "Theokleia tried to get new laws approved in the city so that any fugitive, regardless of the circumstances, could be seized and punished again. Fortunately, she has not been able to make any changes in the way the governor rules the city."

I thought about the day Thekla was to be burned. "I heard that Theokleia had bribed the court to get the punishment she wanted. After the storm that freed Thekla, there never was any official search for her. With the excessive storm damage in the city, no one had time or energy to spare in order to search for her. Months have passed and most people have forgotten the episode. The only one with a grudge to settle is Theokleia."

Pallas and Acca exchanged a knowing glance. "When Thekla went to visit Paul that night, I didn't get any news until Thekla's message that we had to pack and leave as soon as possible. Gaius told us how Theokleia had her arrested and tried by the tribunal," he said.

Acca spoke in a quiet voice. "From the moment Thekla was born, I knew her mother was determined to destroy her. Theokleia had extensive contacts and was skillful at manipulating people. As long as Abrax was alive, there were limits to how much she could do. The day of the trial, Theokleia had her private guards whip me in the hope of getting further information about both Paul and Thekla. I had the impression that she wanted to send men after him when he was thrown out of Iconium. The storm delayed her plans."

I wondered how long it had been since the guards had come through, but didn't get a chance to ask and decided to discuss it further with Pallas later. For now, the conversation now had dampened everyone's mood.

We dropped the subject and considered what we would do for the rest of the day. Thekla wanted to sort through her belongings and Acca was eager to help her. I decided to explore the orchards and Pallas said he would show me around. Pallas was of average height, but the way he carried himself and the facial scar indicated that life as a slave had left permanent damage.

We strolled next to the olive grove along the lane leading to the house. The remains of the storm that had assaulted Iconium a couple months earlier were still visible. Telys and Hector were gradually clearing the debris from the fields and orchards, but it was a long process for only two men. Many small limbs were down and larger trees that had been split through the trunk needed to be chopped down.

"Telys and Hector repaired the villa and their house first. They have just begun clearing the orchards and fields, but it will take a long time before things are back to normal," Pallas said.

We waved as we passed the two men filling a wagon with tree limbs that would eventually be chopped to be used for firewood and other needs. Nothing would go to waste.

"Pallas, you told how Theokleia's guards searched the property for Thekla. How long ago was that?" I asked.

He thought for a moment, "I was surprised because it was so long after Thekla left Iconium. It was . . . maybe two weeks later. Does it matter?"

I thought for several minutes. "I don't know. I heard about Theokleia's efforts with the tribunal to get new laws passed regarding fugitives. She is a determined woman and I don't trust her at all where Thekla is concerned."

By this time we had passed the olive grove and entered woods with as much damage as the first orchard. "I like to come here to read because there is a natural clearing in the middle that is quiet and very pleasant. The trees are as shattered as everywhere else, but the meadow in the middle was relatively untouched."

Because there had been no work done to collect debris, our pace slowed. We didn't talk so that we could concentrate on stepping over brambles and fallen branches in the path. As we got to the clearing, I noticed a several boulders in the middle. Over the years, they'd been worn so that they looked like cluster of permanent outdoor cushions. The dips in the surface provided us with comfortable seats.

I chose a lower boulder with a sort of backrest and Pallas found a spot that suited him. As we made our way through the woods, he seemed to withdraw into himself. I waited for him to speak.

"Thekla has changed a lot in these recent months. She looks the same, but her whole disposition has shifted. I know that she has been through a lot with arrests and judgements to kill her, but she is so calm and peaceful. The girl I knew would have been more likely to seek revenge against those who condemned her."

I nodded. "She has been through a lot, but the beginning of the changes came when she first heard Paul. After her father died, there was a gaping hole in her life. Questions, that might have been answered over the years as a natural outcome of their close relationship, were left open. I think she was searching, but unsure of what she sought."

Pallas toyed with a blade of grass. "Losing her father was very hard, made worse by the absence of her mother's involvement. I think it was the first time Thekla had encountered death. She thwarted most attempts to talk about the loss of her father and brother. Paul's sudden arrival next door seized her attention," Pallas said. "It was such a short period of time, only a day or two. I listened to his speeches and expected to discuss them in depth with Thekla in the same way that we had explored the Greek philosophers. I was startled when she left to visit him in prison. We never had a chance to discuss the ideas."

Burdens of regret and sadness weighed heavily on Pallas, but there was nothing I could say to relieve him.

He continued, "I was shocked with the course of events and

Theokleia's role in them. Now, I keep wondering if I might have handled the situation differently or if I might have prevented any of it."

"I understand your concerns, but Thekla has overcome these
obstacles intact. We cannot prevent ones we love from being faced
with difficulties, otherwise they would not have a chance to mature
in their thinking and behavior." My words sounded stiff when what I
wanted was to offer him some solace. I had wrestled with these concerns every day after Thekla left my home. I wanted so desperately to
protect her that it became a physical pain. Relief came slowly as I got
to know Lectra and her way of seeing things. While I wasn't claiming
the new beliefs for myself, I understood a bit better how the followers
made their choices about life.

Seeing the puzzled expression on Pallas's face I tried again, "If
you consider Thekla's life from the vantage point of her new beliefs,
encountering there horrific challenges may have been essential for
her to grow in her faith and move on. The way I understand it, when
an individual is open to guidance from the Spirit, events unfold in
a way that promotes greater understanding of forgiveness and living with love for all. I was surprised to hear her mention Theokleia
last night, but her comments show how deep and encompassing her
beliefs are."

When he spoke again, his frown wasn't as deep as it had been.
"Thekla was such a willful and determined young woman. She was
very judgmental about others. Sometimes, she reminded me of her
mother in the way she analyzed things and worked hard for whatever
she wanted."

"I've never met Theokleia, but I noticed some of those traits as I
got to know Thekla," I said. "Her determination is the same, but she's
much more gentle with others. I don't know if this change is from being arrested and threatened with death or if it's a consequence of her
new beliefs."

"I would use the word 'metanoia' to describe what has happened to her. She seems to have undergone a major personal transformation," Pallas said hesitantly.

"Yes, I agree with you. The new believers associate this kind of change in a person's life with the effect of the Spirit's presence."

That evening, Acca and Thekla joined Pallas and me in the courtyard for our meal. They seemed very pleased with the work that they had accomplished and parcels were stacked by the entrance to be taken to Iconium and, eventually, Seleucia.

Toward the end of the meal, Thekla said, "My plans have changed a bit. As Acca and I worked together, she decided to come with me to Seleucia."

I raised my eyebrows in surprise and looked at Acca.

Her broad smile spoke for itself, then she said, "I have missed Thekla very much. We had never been apart until she was sent to prison and then she was suddenly out of my life completely. I don't want to experience that again. She will not be able to do everything on her own in Seleucia. I can set up and manage her household."

By the expression on his face, Pallas was startled by her decision. He gave a deep sigh. "If you would allow it, I could come with you too. Acca has been good company, but I would like to know more about the new faith way and could probably help out in some way too."

Thekla took their hands and held them as she laughed. "I would love to have you both with me, as long as you remember that you are free to change your mind if things don't work out the way you hope. My life has been so unpredictable that I have no idea what may await us there."

It was a joyful moment and I was happy for them all. For a fleeting moment, I thought about moving to Seleucia with them. There was nothing holding me in Iconium. Abrax was gone and soon Thekla would be on her way. They were the only people who mattered in my life. When I was a slave, I longed to come home to Galatia. Was I ready to move away?

They discussed how to relocate everyone until the plans were set for moving Acca and Pallas to Seleucia with Thekla. The process would involve two stages. First, Acca and Pallas would fetch Thekla at my place when she was ready to leave. With Telys's help, Pallas would buy a wagon and team of horses to pull it. Two days later, Thekla and I returned to Iconium for her to finalize financial matters and pack for Seleucia.

On the Run

As we returned to Iconium, Thekla mentioned several people she wanted to see, including Gaius and Lectra. My mouth fell open when she added Theokleia and Thamyris to the list. When I started to object, she raised a hand to stop me.

"Regardless of her behavior, Theokleia gave me life. I am grateful to her for that."

"But, . . ." I started to object, but Thekla continued as if I hadn't spoken.

"I know she wanted to kill me and would have succeeded if it hadn't been for others who protected me. I must make an effort to see her and let her know that I hold no bad feelings against her."

I was impressed with her thoughtfulness for Theokleia, but concerned that such a visit might not have the outcome Thekla imagined. "There are two things I need to let you know. Gaius wanted to see you as soon as possible when you got back, but we left so quickly for the country that I had forgotten about his request. The other bit of news is that Thamyris died in a freak accident while we were with Queen Tryphaina."

I watched Thekla for some reaction, but there was none.

Then, she said, "I met him only once in my father's office. After he died, Thamyris was always with my mother, so I never had a chance to get to know him."

The day after we got back home, Gaius arrived to meet with Thekla. I was relieved to have him here and hoped that Thekla might change her mind about seeing Theokleia as a result of their discussion. Unfortunately, I had to leave them for a while when my maid told me about a problem in the courtyard.

As I returned to the living room Gaius said, "I'll come with you to Seleucia and help you negotiate for a suitable villa and property. Please let me know if there's any other way I can help."

Thekla smiled and held his hands for a moment. "I am grateful for all your help, Gaius."

From his intense expression as he glanced at me, I knew he expected more problems while Thekla was in Iconium.

Later that evening as we ate a light supper, Thekla told me about her plans. She was very intent on seeing Theokleia. I pushed aside the piece of fruit I had taken for dessert.

"Thekla, when you visit Theokleia, I will see Lectra. In case you need any kind of assistance, perhaps you will be able to get a message to me there."

Her look of surprise told me that she didn't think my efforts were necessary, but she didn't object.

Our walk to her old neighborhood the following afternoon was very pleasant. However, as we parted near Lectra's home, my cold hands indicated my anxiety for Thekla's time with her mother.

Lectra welcomed me warmly and led me to her customary place in the sunny courtyard.

We had not had a chance to catch up with each other for a long time. She plied me with questions about Thekla's experiences and her future plans. The shadows lengthened, but Thekla did not arrive.

"Lectra, when I came here Thekla went to see Theokleia. I hoped that Thekla would join me here after they finished talking," I said.

"You've seemed preoccupied and now I understand," Lectra said. "While you were away, Theokleia sent guards to search for Thekla here. I don't know what she was planning, but it couldn't have been anything good."

"Could your sons watch for her to leave the villa and help her, if she needs assistance? I want to go home and see if, for some reason, she went there directly." I stood and embraced Lectra.

I hurried home to discover that Thekla wasn't there. Deep inside, I was convinced that something awful had happened to her at her mother's villa, but I couldn't think of anything to do. I tried to stay busy as I waited. I had no appetite, but forced myself to eat some bread in case this turned into a long night. Thinking of Gaius, it seemed premature to contact him since I had no idea what might have happened.

Hours later, I was about ready to go to my room and get some rest when I heard Thekla's voice at the front door. Hearing a second masculine voice respond to her, I hurried to the front door. She stood in the hall with an older man wearing filthy rags who leaned on her for support.

"It's all right for you to come in with me. Daphne was a good friend of my father's and she will understand." Thekla's hair had come undone and her toga was torn and dirty. When she saw me, she said, "This is Codros. He was my father's personal servant. Theokleia has been beating him to get any information she can about my father's contacts in the hope that she would be able to find me."

I nodded and beckoned them inside. "Codros, you are most welcome here. There is another room on the opposite side of the courtyard where you will be able to rest comfortably."

"Thank you, lady. My master mentioned your name once, he thought very highly of you."

We left Codros with my servant while Thekla and I went into the atrium.

"Have you had anything to eat?" When she shook her head, I uncovered the fruit and cheese that I'd kept ready for her.

"Codros will need something to eat too. I don't know whether he's badly bruised or has open wounds," Thekla said in a subdued voice.

"I've made sure that he has everything he needs. Now, tell me what happened."

"It was as you and Gaius anticipated. When I stepped up to the front door, a new guard stood there and demanded to know what I wanted. When I said my name, a peculiar look came over his face and he went inside beckoning me to follow him, then gestured for me to wait in the hall. Laughing as she swept out of a room, Theokleia stopped a few feet from me with the guard at her side.

She eyed me carefully and said, 'You have a lot of nerve you brazen hussy and you are a fool. You won't escape your punishment this time. Seize her and put her in the lock down.'

I had no idea what she meant and there was no opportunity to say anything as he grabbed my arm and forced me to keep up with his quick steps. I was unfamiliar with the rooms we passed through and my lost sense of direction when we left the main quarters to enter the cooking area and servants rooms. He stopped at the last closed door and lifted the rod that kept everything inside. He pushed it open and pulled me inside.

'I've heard about you. We'll have some fun later.' He grabbed my breasts and squeezed them hard before leaving.

I heard the rod drop into place. The interior was dark without windows or any source of light so I made my way slowly around the walls using my fingers to find cracks that might be enlarged. There seemed to be no possibility of escape so I sat and waited. Time passed. I prayed for guidance and then paced when I got tired of sitting. Suddenly, there was a scraping sound at the door and it opened slowly.

'Thekla, come quickly. Don't make a sound,' someone said. I couldn't place the familiar voice, but recognized Codros as my father's favorite servant when I got out. 'We have a few minutes to get out while the guard eats. Follow me.'

"Codros no longer had the smooth stride that I remembered. He limped on his right leg and did not move his arms freely. We left the villa through a narrow door that he had rigged to lock itself from the inside once we were out. As soon as we stepped into the street, someone ran toward us and we backed against the wall. Codros stood in front of me. Zeno held a torch close to his face so I could recognize him. He whistled and his brother, Simmias ran around the corner to meet us. Knowing all the back streets, the brothers said they would guide us to your place. Zeno took the lead and guided us to a street that paralleled the one in the front of Theokleia's villa. We hadn't gone far when we heard people running. Zeno grabbed my hand and Simmias pulled Codros into a narrow alley where we waited inside a back gate.

'Don't worry," Simmias whispered. "This is another way into our place. We'll stay here until we're sure that the guards are gone.' He left us and watched for any activity in the street.

I have no idea how long we stood there, but Codros's legs buckled. He was so thin, I wondered if Theokleia had been starving him. Zeno helped him sit down until we could leave. Fortunately, there was no moonlight that might have exposed us. Simmias summoned us with the same whistle his brother had used earlier. Zeno and Simmias took back lanes and narrow passages wandering to the left or right to avoid main thoroughfares. When we reached your street, they told us to go ahead without them. I turned back and waved to them when we came inside."

I gave a deep sigh of relief. Although it was not I that had had a narrow escape, I felt exhausted, and Thekla looked as if she needed rest too.

I stood at the door to my room with the sudden impulse to offer thanks to her God for the fact that she had returned unharmed. But this God who expected so much frightened me. I went into my garden and looked at the shrine I kept for the Unknown God of the Greeks. Could it be the same deity? Despite my need to give thanks, I felt nothing but confusion.

Codros stood awkwardly at the door to the garden wearing the toga and cloak that Theka had worn when she traveled as a man in Myra. He looked much improved from the previous night.

Thekla beckoned to him. "We are all the same. No slaves or owners. Come have something to eat."

He shot a questioning look at me and I smiled. "What she says is true. Please come join us."

When he finished eating, I asked him if Theokleia knew anything about me.

Codros shook his head vigorously. "I never told her anything. When Thekla was born, I promised her father that I would always look out for her. I knew that they visited you often and thought you would be the one to help Thekla in an emergency. Theokleia kept an eye on me and had me followed whenever I went on errands with the hope that I would lead her to Thekla's hiding place. When those efforts didn't work, she began having me beaten and cut my meals. The new guard has only been with her a few days and didn't know my past. I was trying to figure out how to get him away from Thekla when he ordered me to guard her so that he could eat. He had no regard for me and thought I was just a crippled old man that the mistress didn't like."

"So we are all still safe here?" I asked, just to be sure.

"I am the only one that the master trusted fully with his daughter. All of the other servants could be swayed with Theokleia's promises. Only three of us were immune to her ways: Acca, Pallas and me. It was good that they left after Thekla disappeared because the mistress would have made their lives unbearable."

He turned to Thekla and said, "I cannot go back. I will be glad to serve you as I served your father, whatever your future holds."

Thekla reached for his hand and held it as tears welled in her eyes. When she was finally able to speak, she said, "I am grateful to you for all that you have done for me. You are welcome to join us as we move to Seleucia."

Codros's eyes opened wide and he grinned. "That is where I grew up. No one will remember me, but I know my way around."

"As much as I don't want you to leave, it may be best for you to go to Seleucia now," I said. "With your escape and Codros missing from the household, she may scour the city for both of you."

Thekla looked at her hands clasped in her lap. When she looked up, there were tears in her eyes. "I had wanted to remain a little longer, but my presence puts more people at risk. I'll send a message to Acca and Pallas and another to Gaius. As soon as they can get here we will leave."

Gaius arrived that afternoon, before we had a chance to send a message to him. A subdued Thekla greeted him.

Once we were seated in the courtyard, Thekla said, "Gaius, you were right in all your suspicions about Theokleia. I am here, unharmed, because Codros helped me escape last night."

"I've heard about it because she is demanding that a search be done throughout the city to find you both. She wants you caught dead or alive."

Color drained from Thekla's face and Codros nodded as if he had expected her to take such action.

"We have sent a message to Acca and Pallas to come as soon as possible so that we can leave for Seleucia. Codros is coming with us. Do you have the time to accompany us?" Thekla asked.

"Absolutely. We will not take the main roads because this time the governor's men will watch for you. They don't expect you to go to Seleucia, but I don't want to take a chance. I have heard that they are going to focus on Antioch since that is Paul's base of activity now. To make the men more diligent in their search, Theokleia has offered a reward."

"I think you should dress as a man, until you get close to Seleucia. My servants can go to the market for both you and Codros," I said.

"Your group will leave with three men and one woman, Acca. That should add a measure of safety, if you are stopped somewhere near Iconium."

Three days later, when Pallas and Acca arrived, they were delighted to find that Codros was coming with them. Gaius joined everyone toward evening. We had a hearty supper and went to bed early since they planned to leave at dawn.

"I have given some thought to how we might reduce the risk if we are stopped by any soldiers in the vicinity of Iconium. My story is that I'm taking you to my wife's family in Tarsus. My wife packed household goods and is sending more slaves to her sister. This means that, despite the fact that all of you are free, you need to dress and act as servants while we travel."

Just after daybreak, they pulled away from my villa. Although I'd been part of the planning process, I felt as if I had been abandoned. As I worked to get the villa back in order, I jumped at the least unexpected sound from the street thinking that if any problem developed, it would be while the group was still in the region under Iconium's governance.

When the day passed without incident, I wrote to Tryphaina to let her know about Thekla's move to Seleucia. When we were together, we had expected Thekla to have a leisurely transition from one Roman city to the next. Theokleia's actions changed those considerations. Tryphaina would be surprised at how quickly Thekla was forced to move away from Iconium.

Alone

I had heard no more rumors about troops searching for Thekla so I decided to visit Lectra. She had become a trusted friend and I enjoyed the caring atmosphere in her home. Zeno saw me turn the corner to their street and came to meet me. He hugged me as if I were a favorite aunt.

"I'm so glad that Thekla has you for a friend," he said. "Since we met weeks ago, she has like a sister to me."

"Zeno, thank you for helping her and Codros the other night. They would not have made it to my place without the assistance of you and your brother." He smiled warmly as I spoke.

In the courtyard, Lectra was talking to a group of women so I waited were she usually sat. Furniture and cushions were pushed to the walls so that people could move around easily and set up only those things they needed during the day. I enjoyed sitting by the fountain and listening to the water cascade over the pebbles. Peace enveloped me and I had no concern for the length of time I waited.

"Daphne, I'm so glad to see you." Lectra embraced me and asked one of the women to bring us juice. We chatted about various things until after the woman left.

"Have you had any difficulties recently?" I asked.

Lectra gave me a knowing look, "The soldiers have been here twice looking for Thekla and the escaped slave. I understood their first search because we're across the street from Theokleia's villa. The second, was more interesting. Apparently someone suggested that she might have hidden elsewhere during the search and returned later once the soldiers had gone." She was quiet for a few moments. "I trust most of the people here, but so many come in and out during the day that I don't know everyone well. The reward for their capture is tempting."

I gave Lectra's hand a reassuring squeeze. "Your family has been so supportive of Thekla and we are very grateful."

"I hesitate to ask, but is she still in the area?" Lectra spoke softly so that her voice wouldn't carry.

I shook my head. "I think she's in Seleucia now. I'll be sure to let you know when I have definite information. Her former slaves have chosen to go with her. The man who helped her escape Theokleia is originally from that area and will be a great help as they settle in."

Three weeks passed before I received any news of Thekla. Gaius came to see me one afternoon and told me about their journey and finding a place for them in Seleucia.

"When we left Iconium, I had a feeling that we would be stopped somewhere close to the city. Leaving from the smaller southern gate did not draw attention to us, but any movement that day was under careful scrutiny. We'd been traveling for about two hours when I heard galloping horses approaching behind us. I told everyone to follow my lead.

'Halt! Where are your going?" The first one to reach us commanded. The band on his tunic showed that he held higher rank than the one who joined him. When they noticed my cloak that indicated my rank as magistrate in Iconium, they apologized for the inconvenience. 'We are searching for two fugitives from Iconium and need to search your wagon in case they've hidden there.'

"I nodded. When I told them that the slaves and household goods were for my wife's family in Tarsus, they seemed to accept my explanation.

"Unload the parcels." The second one was not as agreeable as the first, but we complied.

I remained astride my horse and commanded Pallas, Codros and

Thekla to unload as the soldiers watched. The second soldier approached Thekla, 'You're a cute boy, but not very strong.' He shoved her against the wagon giving her a chance to slid under it and away from him to keep working on the opposite side near me.

I moved closer to Thekla, but directed my words to the soldiers. 'What's the matter? He and his father are mute. Let me know what you want them to do, if they don't respond to you.' That news seemed to distract them until they could sort through the rest of the wagon and verify that there was no one hiding under the furniture.

'Nothing.' The second soldier said with disgust. 'Let's get going. I would love to win that reward.'

It took some time to get things loaded in a way that would travel well. I noticed that the soldiers looked back a couple times to see what we were doing. Thekla loaded the parcels as diligently as Pallas and Codros. We didn't talk about the incident or change our pace. By nightfall, we were in the area controlled by Seleucia. We chose to camp with the wagon rather than risk encountering other troops at an inn. In the morning, Thekla removed her head covering and pulled a palla from one of the baskets. That simple change removed any possibility that she would be mistaken for a man."

I had been listening carefully to Gaius's description of their encounter and told him about the searches of Lectra's villa.

"Theokleia is intent on harming Thekla. She always has been. Abrax told me about her attempts to destroy Thekla from the time she was born, but I always thought her attitude would change. I never understood Theokleia's obsession." Mystified by her attitude, he shook his head.

"Abrax often talked about her attempts to harm Thekla, but he was confident that the servants would protect her. When I met Codros, I realized that those who worked for Abrax were very committed to protecting Thekla To the point of putting themselves at risk," I said.

"I am relieved that she's in Seleucia," Gaius said.

I agreed. "Tell me about where they are living."

Gaius smiled. "Seleucia is upriver from the coast. On the side of town away from the sea, there was a huge abandoned villa. I heard that after the family died from the plague, no one turned up to claim it. The property itself extends into the hills and has several dry caves. They all liked the place and moved in immediately. Once I registered the property in Thekla's name, there was nothing more for me to do so I came home."

I asked for more details about the villa, but realized that Gaius hadn't investigated it as thoroughly as I'd hoped.

Alone in my courtyard, I had mixed feelings. Of course, I was thrilled for them to find a good location in Seleucia. At the same time, I missed them all. I knew Thekla could not risk returning to Iconium as long as Theokleia was alive. The room in my home that she used was empty - nothing of hers left behind. I couldn't look forward to her return. Although I hadn't spent much time with Pallas, Acca and Codros, I liked them all very much and would miss them too.

Days passed and I felt at loose ends. Would it be enough to visit Thekla in her new surroundings? I recalled my trip to see Tryphaina in Antioch and wondered about making the same kind of journey to see Thekla. The dread of having to leave them prevented me from making plans. Everyone that I cared about was in Seleucia. Why should I stay here?

I didn't dwell on the issue that had started all of these events which was Thekla's commitment to a new faith. While nothing that I'd heard from Lectra or Thekla was objectionable to me, I'd never involved myself in the practices of their way of living. The new beliefs did have a certain appeal for me. I liked the concept that we are all equal and had given careful thought to the possibility of freeing my servants. A life based on love and forgiveness also drew me to it. They talked a lot about Jesus and how he rose from the dead which made me curious. Paul and Thekla both emphasized celibacy for those who were not married. I'd been celibate since Abrax died and had no desire to pursue other partners. Fortunately, I had saved enough money and didn't need to continue working as a hetaera for my livelihood.

A scent of roses enveloped me as a light breeze swept through the garden. Surely there would be roses in Seluecia. If I were to leave Iconium, I needed to free my servants, sell the villa, pack and transport everything I wanted to take. What a daunting challenge! Years had passed since I left Greece and came home to Iconium. The villa was full. Most of the contents would not go with me, but it all had to be sorted. I couldn't do it on my own, or could I.

Time passed so quickly as I worked through my questions and plans, I hadn't realized that darkness had fallen. My servant lit the oil lamps in the garden and brought my evening meal.

Moving On

That night, I slept better than I had in weeks and I awoke full of energy for the day ahead. The feelings of anxiety and dread had haunted me for so long were gone. It was a great relief that Thekla was safe and settled. More than that, however, was the peace I felt about the decisions I had made for my future. I was ready to move to Seleucia.

Hetaerae seldom became close friends because we worked competitively with the same men in the community. Our clientele were usually a stable group, but occasionally a man would transfer his involvement to another, which tested relationships among the courtesans. I knew all of the professional women in Iconium and would approach them first to find out whether anyone was looking for a new home. I preferred to sell it to another hetaera, if I could. A simple message delivered to each of them would be enough to get the word circulating that my villa was available. It took most of the morning to list all of the courtesans and prepare the hand written messages for my servant to deliver.

Over the course of the coming days, I would know whether there was any interest in my villa. In the meantime, I would begin sorting through everything to select those items that I wanted to take with me. This process would take days, maybe a couple of weeks.

I worked through the villa room by room, including the courtyard. There were a lot of things that I didn't want to pack. My hope was to reduce everything to one wagon load.

My face was streaked with dust and I'd just paused for something to drink when my servant told me that Lectra had come. I wiped my face and joined her in the garden.

"Daphne, what is going on?" She asked in a worried voice.

I smiled. "You are the first one to know my decision."

She shook her head before I could continue. "The rumor is flying that you are selling your villa."

Her comment took me by surprise. I had assumed that the hetaera community was rather closed off from the rest of society. "How did you find out?"

"People talk. One of our women heard some servants talking in the market and mentioned it when she got home. I realized that I hadn't seen you in some time and decided to find out if the rumor was true. As I walked through the hall and saw the baskets full of goods, it's apparent that something is happening."

"I wanted to have things further along before I told friends about my plans, but I'm glad that you are here. When Thekla and her friends left, I struggled to be satisfied with my life in Iconium. A long time ago, when I was able to leave Greece, it was important to me to return to my homeland. When I met Abrax, he eventually became my only client. The friendship with Thekla was such an unexpected delight that my life focused on the two of them. Losing Abrax was hard, but made easier because of my relationship with his daughter. I never thought the day would come when I would leave Iconium, but her move to Seleucia made me think about why I stayed here."

Lectra's eyes filled with sympathy. "I had no idea."

"I finally decided that I am comfortable with Thekla's new beliefs and that I really want to be with her and her friends. Knowing how hard it is for courtesans to find a place to live, I sent messages to each of them in case they or someone they know wants to buy my villa."

"Now I understand, and am relieved. Although I enjoy knowing you, it makes sense that you want to live near Thekla. How can we help?"

"Lectra, you and your family have done so much for Thekla already, that I don't want to impose on you."

She smiled and shook her head. "It's no imposition. I noticed that you seem to be sorting through your belongings. Unless you've made plans to sell everything, I would be glad to take whatever you don't want for some of the women who come to us with nothing. Once you know what you want to leave behind, Zeno and Simmias can come fetch things."

"I've been so intent on selecting what I want for Seleucia that I hadn't begun to think of what I would do with the things that are leftover. I don't want to bother with trying to sell these things. If someone else can use them, I'm glad to pass them on."

Lectra nodded. "Do you know when you will move?"

"I haven't even told Thekla about my decision yet. I was waiting to see how difficult it would be to sell my villa. No one has shown any interest yet and that will determine my schedule."

"Of course." A broad grin spread across Lectra's face as she said, "When you know your timetable, let me know. It would be nice for us to get away from Iconium for a while and I'd love to see Thekla again. Our family could help you move."

Her suggestion took me by surprise and solved a problem I hadn't begun to wrestle with. "I'll be sure to let you know so that we can plan the trip together."

That night, I thought about Lectra's visit and her offers. A sense of peace descended on me and I knew that I was doing the right thing by moving to Seleucia. Ways were opening unexpectedly before me to solve issues I hadn't considered. Surely Thekla's God was approving my actions. I raised my eyes to the stars and gave thanks.

Zeno and Simmias made regular visits to my home. They seemed to enjoy the errand, even when I had nothing ready for them. I always took a break whenever they appeared. Zeno, on the verge of becoming a man, was slightly taller than his younger brother and had a darker complexion. He had the distinctive nose of his mother which combined well with his angular facial features.

One day Zeno looked at me carefully and said, "I'm glad that you will live near Thekla. Mother likes you very much, but she can always visit. You need to be with Thekla."

His perceptive comment surprised me. It seemed like another indication from Thekla's God that I was following the right path.

Then I heard him murmur to himself. "I wish I could be closer."

The wistful sound in his voice reminded me that he was drawn to Thekla. It was probably a good thing that he lived in Iconium and not closer to her. I wondered if he knew that she was committed to remaining celibate.

The second week after my announcement to the hetaera community that my villa was for sale brought an offer to buy it. My neighbor across the street had an apprentice who was looking for a place of her own. After they toured my villa, the apprentice decided to buy it. I accepted the offer and told them that once the fee was paid, I would have a city magistrate register the villa in her name.

The following morning, I sent a letter to Gaius requesting his help to transfer the ownership of my villa. Four days later, he came to my home. Wearing a puzzled expression, he greeted me and we sat down together in the living room, which was the only room that I had saved until last to sort through.

He looked at me intently as if searching for any sign of a problem. I smiled and said, "Gaius, everything is fine. I delayed letting you know about some decisions I've made until my plans became firm."

He raised his eyebrows in question, but didn't interrupt.

"When you accompanied Thekla to Seleucia, I questioned my life in Iconium. The answers that surfaced made me realize that I want to live close to her. I sent word to my professional colleagues that my villa was for sale. My neighbor's apprentice offered to buy it last week. She gave me the payment in full yesterday. I have promised to have her name registered as the new owner, but I don't know what is involved."

Gaius took a deep breath. "This is great news. So many times you and I have met and there has been some difficult problem to solve with little time to do it. This is a pleasant task and I will let you know what fees the city requires when I've finished the paperwork. What else do you need for your move to Seleucia?"

I explained that Onesiphorus's family was going to go with me and visit Thekla during my move. Once the registration for the villa had been changed, I would be on my way.

Adventure

Although Onesiphorus and his family drove up with the wagon shortly after dawn, it took us until mid-morning to get my belongings securely packed with adequate space for us to take turns riding. Lectra and I climbed on top of the parcels and her husband and sons led the way out of Iconium. I'd been looking forward to the journey and felt the tension in my shoulders ease a little more with each mile.

Early in the afternoon, we stopped by the road to eat and allow the horses to graze.

"This will be a short day to avoid being out after dark. We know some farmers not far from here and I'll ask them to let us spend the night with them," Onesiphorus said.

"I appreciate your planning, but isn't there a village where we could find accommodations at an inn rather than impose on your friends?" I asked.

Lectra patted my arm reassuringly and answered, "We've heard that soldiers and other bands of men still roam the countryside looking for Thekla and Codros. As long as the reward is unclaimed, people will search for them. It would be safer for us to stay with friends."

I had become so involved with my plans for selling the villa and leaving Iconium that I hadn't paid attention to any rumors that might have been circulating about those perceived to be on the run from Roman justice. Thanks to Gaius, each of my servants carried documents verifying their freedom. With Thekla and Codros 'safely' in Seleucia, my need to be constantly alert for roving bands in the region had subsided.

Just as the sun was setting, we turned down a lane, with newly sown fields of winter grain on both sides, toward a villa. The owner, a dark, rugged looking man came out and called to his family to join him. They welcomed us warmly and ushered us inside.

"We need to secure the wagon before we relax," Onesiphorus said to our host, Abas who summoned a servant and directed him to drive the wagon behind the villa where it wouldn't be seen.

As we ate, we explained that I was moving to Seleucia and that Onesiphorus's family was helping me. Then, Onesiphorus asked for their news.

Abas shot a quick look at the entrance before speaking. "Last week two soldiers came here and demanded to search the buildings, including every room of the villa. I asked them what they were looking for and they mentioned an escaped criminal and a slave. When they entered our servants' quarters, I waited outside and overheard them discuss splitting a reward. They took hours to check everything and even walked into the fields." He shook his head in disbelief. "I can't imagine why they needed to see the fields."

We all laughed at the idea, but gave no hint that we knew who the guards were searching for. I had learned that it was better to say less than give people information that might put you at risk later. Hearing Abas describe the search made me more eager to get to Seleucia.

Despite using modern Roman roads, the journey took us over a week. We were not concerned with soldiers looking for Thekla and Codros, but with other roaming bands of thieves. Whenever possible we stayed in a village inn or at a farm, but there were a few times when we slept out in the open. Traveling with the wagon meant that we couldn't move far off the road to conceal our presence so Onesiphorus and his sons took turns keeping watch at night. Lectra and I prepared our meals building small fires with collected branches and twigs.

I noticed a gradual transition in plants and trees as we neared the coast. There were fewer fields of grain and more trees, especially citrus. Two days later, the scent in the air changed to a distinct briny odor letting us know that we were close to the sea. Rounding a hill, we made a rapid descent toward the coast. All of us walked except Onesiphorus, who struggled to keep control of the wagon.

What a beautiful sight! The deep blue of the Mediterranean sea was dotted with Roman galleys and fishing boats. We found a good place to pause and refresh ourselves before continuing south to the mouth of Calycadnus river. There we found a fishing village and small inn where we could spend the night before pushing inland to Seleucia.

Our last day took longer than we anticipated as the heavily traveled road followed the curves of the river. It was close to sunset when we finally reached the gate to Seleucia, where Onesiphorus asked for directions to an inn. Gaius had told us that Thekla's villa was on the opposite side of the city, further upriver. The challenge of maneuvering through the city streets and following the river was better suited for daylight.

Now, I sent a message to Thekla that we would be arriving around midday. All of us had slept later than usual and lingered over our food. Soon, I heard someone call my name and stood up. Codros smiled broadly as he spotted us. I marveled at how he had changed in a few weeks. In Iconium, he looked much older and crippled. Now he stood tall with a muscular build and tanned skin.

After he greeted everyone, we headed for the wagon where he easily climbed up and took the reins. He turned to us and said, "Thekla is delighted that you are here. We decided that it would be easier for you if I showed you the way to the villa."

Codros drove the wagon through town, a task complicated by throngs of people and livestock coming to the market. I followed behind walking with the others and trying to absorb everything since this would be my new home. Finally, we passed through another city gate and followed the road with the river on our right. It seemed like we'd gone a very short distance when Codros turned into a lane that was little more than a footpath. He gave a shrill whistle as we rounded a copse of trees and entered the property through a beautiful wooden gate that opened slowly for us. Codros motioned for us to go ahead of the wagon.

As I stepped inside, Thekla ran across the open yard followed by Acca and Pallas. We hugged each other and laughed with delight. Then, she greeted the others hugging them in turn.

"Come." She gestured for us to follow her. Onesiphorus and his sons helped Codros and Pallas move the wagon and unhitch the horses.

Following Thekla, I scanned the villa and was astonished at its size. We passed through the atrium to a huge courtyard with a large pool in the center. Columns ascended to the roof above the second floor. In front of each pillar was an urn filled with flowering plants and vines that wrapped around the columns.

"Thekla, this place is enormous!" I exclaimed.

She grinned. "We all favored this place more than any other that we saw. It had been abandoned for a long time and needed a lot of repairs. Codros found people he had known when he was young and they helped us restore the place quickly." She waved her arms around and said, "There's plenty of space for all of you for as long as you want to stay. After we eat, we'll show you around."

There was a blossoming citrus tree in the far corner of the courtyard that scented the air with a pleasant tang. Cushions had been arranged for us around a low table filled with baskets of bread, roasted meat and fruit where the four of us women sat and waited for the men to come inside.

"How was your trip?" Thekla asked.

Lectra shook her head and said, "It took much longer than I expected. I thought the two cities were closer to each other."

"The views of the sea as we descended to the coast were spectacular," I said. Unexpectedly, the memory of Abas's farm flashed through my thoughts. I decided to tell Thekla what we had learned from him.

"We didn't have any trouble anywhere, but the first night we learned that soldiers and others bands of men are still searching for you and Codros in the region under Iconium's jurisdiction. As long as the reward goes unclaimed, I think people will keep looking."

Thekla smiled. "It's good to know what's going on, but I have no plans to leave here and I doubt that Codros has any interest in seeing Iconium again. Since we arrived he has found a few people that he knew as a child. I think he's happy to be home."

Acca saw the others come in and waved for them to join us. We ate as if we hadn't been fed that morning. Once our hunger was sated, we rested against the cushions until Zeno and Simmias got up, declaring they were going to explore outside.

"Wait boys, we may still need your help," Onesiphorus said. "Thekla, where should we store Daphne's things until she finds a home?"

Thekla looked at me. "This villa is huge. I would love to have you stay here. You've been a cherished friend to me and I have missed you very much." She put her hand on my arm as if she feared I would disappear. Then, she smiled and said. "We have chosen the rooms we want to use, but two of the wings are still empty as well as most of the second floor. If you decide that you still want to be on your own, you can always move into the city later. Let me know what you think after you've had a chance to look around."

Her comments touched me and I blinked to avoid spilling tears. How I'd longed to be with her. But, I'd been living alone for years and wasn't sure I could adjust to someone else's living arrangements."I'll give it a try. If it doesn't work you can help me find a place nearby." I turned to Onesiphorus and said, "Why don't you just enjoy the rest of the day and we'll figure out what to do tomorrow."

Zeno and Simmias were on their way before I finished speaking. Pallas and Codros took Onesiphorus with them for the afternoon. Thekla laughed and clapped her hands.

"That leaves us to ourselves. Come, I'll show you the villa. We'll start upstairs."

The stairs near where we were seated partially obscured the back rooms. As we climbed to the second floor, I noticed that most of the rooms were completely empty. At the front of the villa above the entrance, Thekla motioned for us to enter and I knew immediately by the way the furniture and curtains were arranged that these were her rooms.

She paused at a window seat. "I love to sit here and watch the birds in the trees. You can even get a glimpse of the river in the distance."

The light was perfect and the view wonderful, but I preferred to be on the ground. We took a second staircase that ended by the front door. Pallas and Codros had their rooms on either side of the entrance with Pallas's quarters to the right and Codros on the left. The wings along the sides were normally unoccupied, but two rooms had some bedding for Onesiphorus, Lectra and their sons. Another room across the courtyard had been set up for my use.

We approached the tree again where we'd eaten and Acca said, "The rooms in the back here are mine. They make it easy for me to continue working the way I did when Thekla was young. I enjoy preparing meals and caring for the villa."

Now Thekla led us outside to show us a storage building with stalls for animals. There was evidence of vegetable and flower gardens but these hadn't been reestablished yet. I loved gardening and these spaces had been well placed for sunlight and drainage. My fingers itched to begin working in them.

Beyond the front gate paths led in several directions. Thekla took us to the citrus grove with lemon and orange trees. "Another path would take us to the olive grove and grapevines. There is so much here that we haven't begun to develop. Our efforts have been to get the villa repaired. I don't know whether we will get the orchards and vineyard going again or just use whatever happens to bear fruit. Pallas and Codros have some ideas they're working on. It takes a lot of time to clean up, repair and prune."

I looked at Thekla and asked, "What is your favorite part?"

"You haven't seen it yet. There's a grotto with a dry cave. I'm aware of the Spirit there more than anywhere else. I spend hours there in prayer and listening for guidance. Having received this wonderful place, I know that much is expected of those of us who believe."

I thought about Pallas, Acca and Codros, then asked, "Has everyone accepted the new teachings about love and forgiveness?"

She smiled. "Pallas has adopted the new faith. Acca and Codros are exploring what it means to leave the old gods behind."

Lectra had been quiet until now. "When people come to us, they have already have taken the most difficult step to pursue a new way of living. Everyone is different in how they find their path to love and forgiveness."

There was a fallen branch and some large rocks in the shade where we could sit. When we were comfortable, Thekla looked at Lectra and continued the conversation.

"How did you start your work in Iconium?"

Lectra took a deep breath and thought for several minutes. "Once I realized that there was a need for people to have a meeting place, it seemed natural to invite them to our home. Things tend to change according to how many people are with us and the concerns that they have. Basically, everyone tries to help each other. The villa may belong to us, but the work is sustained by everyone there. Don't worry about making it happen here because the Spirit will open the way for you when it's right for the next phase of your work to unfold."

My mind was pulled in too many directions to focus on their conversation as they discussed more details about how the work proceeded for Onesiphorus and Lectra. I thought about what Thekla had shown us in the villa, gardens and orchards. The place attracted me so strongly that I felt the urge to unpack, but I wasn't sure that it was the right thing for me to do. Could I find a place in town and come out to help in the gardens or should I try living here? Maybe if I stayed here a few days I would be able to figure out the answer.

I had avoided thinking too much about my own lack of faith in Roman and Greek gods or what involvement with the new beliefs might mean for me. To live grounded in love didn't seem too hard, but I harbored strong hostility against the men who had sold me into slavery as a child. If I fully accepted the new way of life, I'd have to let that go and I didn't know if I could manage to forgive them, yet.

The next day, Onesiphorus and his family walked back to town. When I chose to stay at the villa, Thekla asked me to accompany her to the cave. She gave me a skin of water to carry and she took some bread and cheese, so I knew we would be gone for most of the day.

What began as an easy stroll soon changed to an uphill climb on a rock strewn path. We stopped often to enjoy the sight of the river below and views of the forests all around. Our path gradually wound between boulders until it seemed that we were walking on solid rock. Thekla made an abrupt turn to the right and descended a series of stepping stones to a grassy area where I thought we would stop, but Thekla continued up a narrow trail on the other side. The climb was steep, and I was grateful when Thekla stopped. I'd been paying close attention to where I stepped and hadn't looked around.

She waved her arm in an arc and said, "Look, isn't this beautiful?"

To our right was a small dry cave and to the left was the grassy area below. The most spectacular sight, however, was the river beyond the trees.

"Come, I want to show you the cave before we sit down," she said.

The opening was broad with a shelf that jutted out above the grotto below. Inside there was a dry, smooth dirt floor that had been covered with mats and cushions. Small niches in the walls held oil lamps and other items. She grabbed two cushions and pulled them into the sun outside.

"This is my place. Here I can be close to the Spirit and hear her guidance. I spend a lot of time here and the others know to come to the cave whenever I'm not at the villa."

I looked all around and felt at peace with life and the world. I turned to Thekla and said, "I can understand why you like to be here. I'm glad you found such a wonderful place that suited all of you."

With a twinkle in her eyes, she asked, "And what about you? Will you settle here at the villa with us?"

It was hard to resist the attraction I felt for the place. There were so many things that appealed to me. My greater concern was how I would fit with their beliefs. "I do like your villa and the land very much. It draws me to it, especially your gardens." I paused and took a deep breath. It was difficult to describe what was holding me back. "I'm reluctant to move in because I'm unsure of how your new beliefs affect daily routines. I am not against the new ways, but I'm not sure I understand them."

Thekla smiled and gave my hand a quick reassuring squeeze. "I understand your concern about our beliefs, but there's nothing set in stone. The Spirit has found each of us in a different way. No one can dictate beliefs to another, it has to be as one searches for and yields to the leading of the Spirit. We often offer prayers of gratitude for what is provided to us. We seek guidance for our activities and major decisions. There are no rules, as such. We try to live each day as an expression of love and forgiveness as Jesus taught his followers."

"But don't you have to give some kind of offering or tribute?" I asked. "All of the gods and goddesses I've heard about require financial support and gifts."

"No," Thekla said shaking her head. "It is the way we try to live that is our constant offering to the Creator. Living together in this way, we have become very aware of each other's needs and safety.

That loving awareness makes us take care of all that has been given to us, including each other, as well as how we manage the buildings and the land. We know that our way of life is threatening, especially to those in power. We try to live according to the rules of the larger community, but no other human being holds power over us. This attitude is frightening to many."

I didn't know how to reply because deep inside I felt a strong resonance with everything she said. Life as a hetaera was lived on the fringes of society, so that part didn't frighten me, but I didn't know if I had the courage to face the trials that Thekla had lived through.

"Daphne, I think the only sure way you can find the answers to your questions is by living with us for a couple of months. Then, if you find that you must move into a place of your own, we'll help you."

I looked into her eyes as she spoke and then nodded slowly. "I'll try it. We can unpack the wagon."

Thekla hugged me. "I'm so glad. When we go back to the villa you can choose your rooms."

The sun was high overhead. Seated in the sun, we had become very warm and developed a thirst. Thekla grabbed her skin of water and took a drink before opening the small sacks she had carried. We spread bread and assorted fruit on the cloth.

Thekla lifted her arms and prayed. "Thank you for the gift of friendship. Bless us as we live and work together. Bless the food you have provided."

When we finished eating and had wrapped the remaining fruit and bread, Thekla said, "Whenever you have questions about the new beliefs or the Spirit, feel free to ask. We are all followers of these beliefs, but we have had different experiences with the Spirit's guidance. You may want to talk to the others too for their insights about how they adopted the new way."

I needed some time to myself and decided to explore the grotto below. Thekla stayed outside the cave. The woods around the small grassy meadow were difficult to move through. I had to maneuver around downed branches and dense brambles if I wanted to go deep into the woods. I gathered a few wild flowers that grew in the shade and some dazzling poppies and daisies blossoming in full sunlight. How nice it would be if I could transplant them in the gardens at the villa.

Eventually, I heard the clatter of stones and noticed that Thekla was coming toward me.

"I'm ready to go back," Thekla said. I took my water skin and one of the sacks from her as we climbed up the way we came.

After dinner that night, Zeno and Simmias described Seleucia in great detail, especially the market where Onesiphorus and Lectra bought citrus to take home. Lectra also found some baskets that were woven in a different design from the ones we were accustomed to in Iconium.

"I hate to mention it, but we need to go home soon," Onesiphorus gave a meaningful look to Lectra.

She said, "We've left our villa in the care of those who live with us. I don't want to stay away too long."

I looked at them all. "You have been so kind to help me move to Seleucia. I am very glad to have you as my friends. Tomorrow morning, we can unload the wagon so that you can fill it with your purchases and get on your way whenever you're ready."

Lectra's eyes opened wide as she looked at me. "So, you've decided to stay here?"

"Yes. If I'm meant to stay here, things will work out. If not, I can move into town."Everyone started talking at once. Acca leaned over and hugged me. Pallas and Codros said they would help me set up my rooms. Thekla leaned into her cushions with a broad grin as she took in everything.

My New Home

Everyone woke early the following day, eager to begin emptying the wagon. As soon as Onesiphorus had it rearranged to his satisfaction, he was ready to go. Lectra hugged each of us and the boys hugged me too.

When I was sorting my belongings in Iconium, I'd gotten to know Zeno and Simmias. Now, I watched Zeno approach me and realized that he was gaining the features of a man. His muscles were more developed and his face more angular than before. He stood before me and hesitated. "I'm sorry to say good-bye to you because I've enjoyed being with you on the trip here and before at your villa. I hope I can get back to Seleucia some time."

His comments surprised me because I didn't realize I'd made any impression with either of them.

When Lectra heard him, she said, "I'm sure we'll have an opportunity to visit Seleucia again."

I saw Zeno walk over to Thekla and take her hand. I don't know what was said, but she smiled in response. Then he climbed into the wagon.

Seated in the wagon, Onesiphorus called to the others to climb on. With a nearly empty wagon, everyone could ride.

When the wagon was out of sight, Codros closed the gate to the villa. Then he turned to me and said, "Let's get started on your rooms. Which ones do you want to use?"

I led him to rooms away from the entrance, in the wing on the side facing the garden. These windows opened directly to the gardens while the opposite wing offered views of the orchard. Pallas joined us as I explained how I wanted to set up one room as a bedroom and the other as a sitting room. Soon they were hauling furniture, chests, and baskets. Thekla and Acca helped me unpack, hang curtains, and arrange cushions. We stopped for a break at noon to eat. After a short rest, the three of us women finished setting up my rooms.

That night, I was happy to snuggle into my own bed. Dreamless sleep came quickly.

In the morning, I heard the others talking in the courtyard, and I joined them for breakfast.

Acca passed me some bread and said, "Each of us has chosen something that we enjoy doing here. Is there something that appeals to you?"

Thekla laughed knowingly and I grinned. "It's no secret that I love gardens. I noticed that no one has claimed them so I'll be glad to see what I can do."

Codros wiped his brow in an exaggerated manner. "That's a relief because I don't like to work in the dirt. If you hadn't come, Daphne, I'm afraid taking care of the garden would have ended up on my list." The others laughed at him.

I gave him a meaningful glance. "Would you be willing to help me once in a while?"

"Sure," Codros paused. "As long as it doesn't happen too often." Everyone laughed again, knowing that he readily helped out wherever he was needed.

Now that my rooms in the villa were set up, it was time to see what I might need to clear out and replant in the gardens. Codros showed me where tools and outside baskets were stored so that I chose whatever I needed. The baskets filled quickly with debris and he hauled them away to burn the trash. When I needed a break, I stood next to him and watched the fire.

"Codros, I almost didn't recognize you that morning when you came to guide us to the villa."

He tossed a handful of twigs on the fire and turned toward me with a broad smile. "I'm not the same person. Being free again and in my own homeland has renewed me in ways I never imagined, lady."

"Please call me Daphne. My past experiences are similar to yours. I was born in Galatia, but was captured and sold as a slave in Greece when I was a child. When I gained my freedom, I learned to make my own way in the world."

A wave of astonishment scrolled across Codros's features. "Abrax always held you in high regard. Despite the fact that he was my master, I thought he was a remarkable person because he dealt with everyone as if he or she were his equal. He wasn't naive, but had seen enough of life to know how quickly one's circumstances could change."

I scanned the villa and the outbuildings. "He would have been proud of his daughter's accomplishment."

"I agree with you. I think he would have found the new beliefs appealing too, as I do."

His open statement about the new faith way surprised me. I wanted to know more from his perspective. There was a twinkle in his hazel eyes when he spoke again. For a moment, I was entranced. Despite his firm jaw and rugged appearance, a deep kindness softened his features drawing me to him. He was at peace with himself and exuded a calming influence that enveloped those he was with.

"When you first met me, I'd been starved and beaten for weeks. After our escape, when we hid in the alley, Thekla prayed for my strength to be restored so that I could accompany her to your place. I was slumped on the ground and ready to tell them to go on without me. When Simmias returned, the boys pulled me to my feet and I felt a surge of strength in my arms and legs that I hadn't experienced for weeks. It was still difficult to walk with the other injuries I had, but the new stamina gave me hope that I would be able to recover. Before seeing Thekla again, I'd given up hope, and death seemed better than living in that household."

I gave him a skeptical look. Having never seen a miracle, I didn't know how they worked. I assumed that the momentary rest did more for him than he realized.

"Daphne, the change in my strength stunned me. What was even more remarkable was how quickly I regained my health. The worst bruises healed in a couple days and I could stand up straight again. By the time we reached Seleucia, I was walking normally."

"And you believe this was due to Thekla's prayer?"

"In part." Drawing his brows together in a pensive expression, he continued, "Just being out of Theokleia's grasp and the constant threat of being beaten was a tremendous relief. Eating normally and having time to heal made a difference too. The biggest change was that I felt younger than I had in years, and that feeling of youthfulness has not disappeared."

The fire was nearly out, but I didn't add more dried weeds, because I didn't want to interrupt his train of thought.

"I asked Thekla why she returned to her mother's home knowing she faced a serious risk of being seized or worse. Her answer astonished me; she said that she wanted to tell Theokleia about the new faith and let her know that she was forgiven. Forgiveness? I wondered how she could genuinely forgive Theokleia. That's when she began teaching me about the new beliefs. It's not just her teaching, but that she actually lives accordingly." Codros noticed the fire was almost ashes. He stirred them up and added more fuel.

When he returned to my side, he spoke again. "You asked if Thekla's prayer caused the change in me. I have to say that it was the start of my faith journey that still continues. Jesus is revered as the Life-Giver in the land of his birth. That concept certainly applies to my experience, and I revere him too."

After the morning's exertion, using more muscles than I had in a long time, I stretched out on my bed to rest. The conversation with

Codros provoked me to think more about how the new faith way was affecting different people. Lectra said that each one is drawn to it by the Spirit in the way that is most appropriate for him or her. She went to hear Paul out of curiosity. Did the Spirit trigger that response in her? Lectra didn't have a dramatic story like Thekla's escape from certain death or Codros's run to freedom, but she was firmly committed to the new way of living.

As for me, I only knew that I needed to follow Thekla and the others to Seleucia. That didn't seem to be something of the Spirit, but that I missed her.

That night, after the exertion in the gardens, I fell asleep readily. Dreams carried me away from Seleucia to Iconium.

I stood outside the temple where Thekla had offered gifts to the gods for her father's afterlife. The next thing I knew Abrax was standing with me. "Daphne, move on with your life. Do not mourn for me. If you find someone who cares for you, go with him." He kissed my cheek and walked away.

It was such a vivid dream that I recalled every detail when I woke in the morning. I felt no sadness, but only release. I never imagined a relationship with another man, but Abrax's message suggested the possibility. The thought made me smile.

I worked in the gardens every morning and they were finally showing improvement. Many of the plants had died of neglect.

Codros found me eyeing my work. "Would you like to go to town to see if we can find more plants? I know some people who might be willing to sell some to us."

"When is the best time to go?" I asked. We decided to go the following day mid-morning when the market was fully open and there was less congestion at the city gates.

After breakfast, Pallas asked to come with us to visit the scribes hoping to buy vellum and ink. This was the first time I'd been in the city since we passed through on our way to the villa. I tried to absorb everything, especially the streets we followed to the market. The central square was very congested and Codros took my arm so that we didn't get separated. Pallas had already gone off on his errands and promised to see us back at the villa when he was finished. We skirted the livestock area, but the scent of beasts, offal and slaughter carried on the air. Codros kept his hand on my elbow to guide me through most of the stalls. As we approached the opposite side of the market square, a man from one stall called his name.

"Hello, Kittos," Codros called to his friend, a short, muscular man with unruly dark hair and full beard. "You're just the person we want to see."

Kittos was short and stocky with a swarthy complexion, almost the opposite of tall, fair-skinned Codros. His stall had no awning and the sun highlighted the vibrant colors of his produce and the few plants he had arranged with soil in baskets. Codros introduced me and explained that we were searching for roses and other flowering plants for the gardens at the villa. Kittos showed us what he had on hand and said he could arrange for other plants if we needed them. The ones he had in the stall were thriving and would work well in our gardens. We bought several of them, but I wanted more. He promised to bring an assortment to the villa the following day.

We stopped at a few more stalls to buy fruits and vegetables not grown at the villa. On our way home, Codros told me about his friend.

"Kittos is one of the few people I knew before I became a slave. He inherited his father's farm. It should have gone to his older brother, but he died during the plague. His farm is next to the one my family owned."

I stopped walking and looked at Codros. "Didn't you want to go back to your family?"

He gave a sad smile. "They're all gone now and someone else has the farm. When I was a slave, I daydreamed about coming home and working the land just like Kittos. Over the years, that longing evaporated. My family and most of my friends are gone now. I am grateful that Kittos remembered me."

Hearing him talk, I recalled my reaction when I saw my village for the first time after returning to Iconium. Daphne was much smaller than Seleucia. Nothing looked familiar and all of the families I knew were gone.

Although Codros was much taller than I, he matched his pace to my footsteps and pointed out various trees and plants common to the region. At one point, he stopped by the side of the road and pointed through the branches so that I could get a glimpse of the river.

Kittos arrived as we were finishing breakfast the next morning. We invited him to join us.

After introductions were finished, he looked at each one of us and said, "You're not a family, but you live together?"

Thekla laughed. "Yes, we live together because we follow a new way of life based on love and forgiveness."

Kittos scowled. "Is that legal?"

"Which, that we live together or follow a new faith?"

He scratched his head. "Both, I guess."

Still smiling, Thekla said, "Our arrangements are unusual, but not illegal. We believe in living as if we truly love and care for others. This means that we also strive to forgive those who have done wrong to us."

Codros spoke up. "All of us except Thekla have been slaves at some point in our lives. Thekla's mother had her arrested. We've all lived through difficult situations caused by others, but we have chosen to forgive them."

"I don't understand. Gods and beliefs never had much of an effect on my life," Kittos said shaking his head. "Let's go look at your gardens."

He brought a lot of plants and all of them were healthy and ready for the soil. After we chose the ones we wanted, he sliced the twine holding them together with his knife.

"By Jupiter, help me." Kittos cried and sank to the ground.

He dropped the knife and the plants as blood flowed from his hand. I pulled off my head scarf and covered the huge gash in the palm of his hand, pressing hard in the hope that it would stop bleeding. The cloth was soon saturated.

Codros shouted for Thekla and within moments she ran to us with a handful of cloths.

We bound his hand and tied it securely with a strip from a longer cloth.

When we had finished, Thekla looked up to the sky and opened her arms, "Father-Mother God we ask your help for Kittos. May his hand heal quickly."

Kittos stared at her for a moment, but said nothing. Codros handed him a cup of water which he gulped without taking his eyes off Thekla. When Kittos got up, Codros helped him pack the unwanted plants and accompanied him to his home.

A week later, Kittos returned to the villa again as we were finishing breakfast. He was accompanied by his wife, a mild-mannered woman carrying a basket full of vegetables. He had a large sack slung over his shoulder which he set down in the courtyard before they joined us. He sat next to me and I noticed that his hand seemed to be completely healed.

Codros greeted his friend and his wife, Crisa then said, "I don't know whether we need more plants for the garden."

Kittos shook his head. "We brought some of our harvest and a rose bush as a gift for you."

Crisa brushed curly brown hair away from her eyes and passed the basket to Acca. Then she opened the sack so that we could see that the rose had started to bloom. Kittos held up his palm where there was only a small pale line where he had been cut.

"My hand has healed in just a few days with almost no scar," he said. "I have never had a cut heal so quickly. Whether it was the prayer or the way you bandaged it, I don't know, but I'm grateful."

"My husband told me how you all live together here in harmony. I would like to know more about this new faith," Crisa said.

Thekla led the discussion and asked the others to add their experiences with the new way of living. When Kittos and Crisa departed, Thekla promised to come to their stall the following day and share the teachings with their friends.

This couple's visit marked the beginning of Thekla's work in Seleucia. Until now, we had all been deeply involved reestablishing the property. She was eager to share her spiritual insights of the New Faith with others and maintained a daily schedule including several hours of solitude in her cave to listen for the Spirit's guidance. Until meeting Kittos and Crisa, she seemed to lack direction for how to begin.

The following day, just before midday when the market sales would be slow, Codros and I accompanied Thekla to Kittos's stall. We were surprised to see several people already waiting for us. Kittos introduced us to the others and invited Thekla to address the crowd.

"I've told you about Thekla, the woman who prayed when I cut my hand last week. The wound was very deep and I expected to have a permanent scar that limited the use of my hand. It astonished me when my hand healed very quickly without any complication. The only thing they did differently from what I've done in the past was to pray to their God. Look." He held up his hand so that everyone could see the long pale scar across the palm. "I don't believe in Jupiter or the other Greek gods people talk about. My offerings have never had an impact on my daily life. Thekla's prayer has made all the difference for me so I asked her to come talk to us today."

The small group of market vendors was very attentive. The clothes they wore were functional for their work in the stalls. None was from Seleucia's elite. Grounded in experience and practical application of whatever worked to improve their lives, they accepted Kittos's remarks, but cast a skeptical look at Thekla. One man grabbed Kittos's hand and rubbed his finger over the scar.

Thekla smiled as she looked at the gathering. "What Kittos has told you about his wound is true." She gestured in my direction and said, "Daphne and I took care of Kittos last week. The cut bled excessively making it hard to bandage his hand. The only thing I did after we finished was that I prayed to our Father and Mother God. I am an apostle teaching a new way of living in love and forgiveness that was first taught by the Life-Giver Jesus. He lived according to his teachings and today those who follow him try to live in the same way. Jesus' earthly life ended with his crucifixion, but he taught us about his boundless love and forgiveness. The change in my life and for other believers has been truly life giving."

"What's the name of his god?" A man in the back shouted. "Seleucia is known to be a center for worshiping Jupiter, and his temple is here."

Thekla opened her arms as if to embrace everything she saw. "Jesus referred to God as our parent, our father and mother. No name is needed because we can pray to our divine parents. They created human beings as brothers and sisters to love and help each other. Together with loving others, we need to forgive them whenever they make a mistake. Jesus forgave the men who crucified him as he hung from the cross. We are meant to forgive others the way he did."

A hush fell over the people as they listened.

"It's hard to believe that this Jesus would do something like that, forgive those who crucified him. I would curse them with my last breath," the man next to me said.

Thekla looked at him and nodded. "I understand what you are saying. But, from my own life experience, I know that forgiveness is important for each of us. Who has not made a mistake that had a disastrous outcome? Who has not been damaged in some way by another? The memories of these experiences come back to us again and again with the least provocation from other events, long after the damage has been repaired. To stop carrying that memory and being hurt repeatedly by it, we must forgive."

The man shrugged and shook his head. Thekla looked around at the others.

"Sometimes it takes a while to understand that forgiving another's bad action toward you ultimately helps you to be fully alive." Her face glowed as she spoke. "We are created to be equal, not to be slaves or possessions of another."

One fat man looked at the person next to him who was very thin and laughed. "We don't look equal."

The crowd joined in his laughter.

Thekla grinned. "Outward appearances deceive. Consider that we are all created to be human beings. That is our common bond. Just as you care for and help your family, remember that every person you see has been created to be your brother or sister. We live most successfully when we love and help each other."

The same man called out. "That won't make you rich!"

Thekla answered, "Do riches matter so much when everyone is meant to be your family to help you? In sharing whatever we have with each other, we are blessed and rich in ways we seldom think about."

"Where is the temple for this new God?" A woman asked.

"God needs no temple because all creation is a temple. We can worship wherever we are because God is always with us."

Other people had stopped to listen to the discussion and the crowd drew the attention of the soldiers who began shoving people and telling them to make way for people to pass. There was a distinct change in the atmosphere and I began to worry that the soldiers' roughness would precipitate conflict.

"If you want to hear more about the new beliefs, I will come back again next week." As she spoke, she glanced at Kittos, who nodded. "Go in peace and let love guide you."

I watched Thekla as she spoke to others and handled their comments. Her arms seemed to enfold everyone as she leaned into the crowd with a sincerity seldom demonstrated in a public setting. What a remarkable person she had become. Her physical beauty caught everyone's attention, but the musical quality of her voice and the ideas she presented made people crowd closer to her. I was proud of who she had become and, despite having known her since childhood, I too, was captivated by her teaching.

The group dispersed and Crisa invited us inside their stall. She poured wine for us and Kittos opened a sack of bread. As was her habit, Thekla offered a brief prayer of thanksgiving for our hosts and their food.

Codros seemed to be lost in his thoughts as we walked home that afternoon. He stopped when we turned into the lane for the villa, and said, "Thekla, I heard people asking how they could find you. It made me wonder how you want to work in Seleucia. Teaching at Kittos's stall is fine as long as it doesn't interfere with his sales, or draw too much attention of the soldiers and other merenaries. Another possibility might be for people to come to the villa to hear you. Have you given any thought to where you want to teach?"

"I always taught with Paul in the market place. Today is the first time that I've taught on my own and dressed as a woman."

I looked at her carefully and asked, "Was it harder to teach alone, as a woman?"

"It's hard to say. I noticed the men eying me in a way they didn't when I taught as a man. It made me uneasy, but I was determined to teach as well as I could. Today's experience convinces me that I need to find another place that is less public."

As we walked, I thought about Lectra's home that was open to all believers all the time and didn't know whether I could live that way. The questions Codros asked needed to be sorted out, but I felt uneasy about the possible outcome. Perhaps I had moved into the villa too quickly. A glance at Thekla's expression told me that she was pondering the events of the day very carefully.

I thought all of us might sit down and discuss the need for a place where Thekla could teach when we returned to the villa, but Pallas and Acca were involved in lengthy projects and unable to stop. As a result, it wasn't until the next morning that Thekla shared her thoughts on where she would prefer to teach.

"In the past, my teaching has always been done in public places. Those were good learning experiences for me, but not the way I would like to work here in Seleucia. I would like to find a way to teach in the grotto below the cave, but I'm not sure how to arrange that." Thekla looked at us with an expectant expression, anticipating some suggestions.

Her choice surprised me. "Are you sure? I know it's a special place for you. Do you really want to have everyone coming and going there?" The others nodded as I spoke.

"I think it would be ideal because it is away from the city crowds and would allow routines to continue at the villa without interruption," Thekla said.

"With some help, I think that Pallas and I can fix the grotto for you. We need to hire a few men to expand the area in front of the cave and open a direct path from the road to the grotto. I'm sure there will be other things that need to be done once we get started," Codros said with a glance at Pallas, who nodded his agreement.

Thekla smiled. "We should put the outline of a fish at the entrance to the path leading to the grotto. This is the symbol that many followers use to show the way to meeting places for believers of the new faith."

Acca put a comforting hand on Thekla's arm and said, "Explore that cave with Codros to see if it can be extended further into the hill-side. You may be spending a lot of time there and should have a private area where you can rest."

Thekla looked at me with her eyebrows raised in question.

"All of these ideas sound good to me," I said. "I have always been concerned for you teaching in the market place. The risk to you from hecklers and others who disapprove of the new faith way is too great. If people must choose to find you in the place you have selected, the situation is better for everyone. I agree with Acca that we need to make the cave more comfortable for you so that you can take advantage of the solitude you find there. If it can be extended into the hill, perhaps we can partition the deeper section with a curtain to be your personal space for rest and prayer."

Thekla's eyes twinkled. "I have only one question, when can we start?"

"Let's find a time that we can all go to the grotto with you. Then we can ask questions and each of us can find out what we need to do," I suggested. "Even if everything isn't completely finished, it would be good if the major work were done by the time Thekla is scheduled to teach next week. Kittos could let people know where to come."

That afternoon, we followed Thekla to the grotto. Codros and Pallas walked the periphery of the open space with her to see where the seating could be extended. While they marked a path to the main road, Acca and I went into the cave with Thekla.

"I would like a few more oil lamps and cushions." Thekla pointed to the spots where they should be added. She walked to the back wall and said, "If Codros can add another area, I would keep some fruit and water here, too."

The work required careful thought. Thekla, Acca, and I headed to the grotto every morning carrying various supplies to make the cave more comfortable. The men focused their efforts on creating the path from the main road.

A few days, later close to sunset, there was some commotion at the gate as Pallas met Gaius who had arrived on horseback. He dismounted and greeted everyone as Pallas led the horse away.

"How wonderful to see you all again. I must admit that I have wondered how things have developed here and it looks like everyone is doing very well," he said, taking everything in. "The villa and gardens look much better than when I saw them for the first time."

Acca ran ahead of us to finish dinner preparations. Inside the courtyard, Gaius continued to examine the repairs before we gathered in the far corner under the tree to eat. As had become our custom, I sat between Thekla and Codros. I'm not sure how our seating arrangement came to be, but once started, we all kept to our places. The spot directly across from Thekla was usually reserved for guests and Gaius took a seat there.

After dinner, Thekla asked, "What news do you have for us?"

Gaius reached into the folds of his toga and pulled out a scroll. "Lectra sent this to Daphne, but the contents are not secret. When she asked me to send the letter, she didn't think that I would be the one to bring it. She told me that she chose her words carefully without mentioning names in case it fell into the wrong hands. I thought about her letter and decided that since I had some free time, I wanted to see everyone again. I like this place and have wondered how your repairs and improvements were progressing."

He passed the scroll to me and I opened it immediately. After scanning its contents, I read it to the others.

Dearest friend Daphne,

Our return to Iconium went smoothly without any unusual encounters on the way home. Much to our surprise, however, our villa had been searched twice while we were away. Now the house and street are under constant surveillance, especially from our neighbor's place. Apparently, we are suspected of either harboring criminals or enabling them to escape the city.

While the soldiers do not seem to be actively searching for escaped slaves or convicts, news of the reward for their capture has become general knowledge. Several men have formed teams to continue the search here, and beyond Iconium, in the hope of receiving the cash. They have no official orders to seize people, but take their own initiative to create havoc. I have no idea how far these men have spread and anyone who has lived in Iconium is at risk of being seized. Upstanding, innocent people are being apprehended by these greedy rogues.

I think these mercenaries will eventually be stopped as the uproar about innocent people being mistreated increases. My concern is for the unsuspecting people that they seize beyond Iconium. Hopefully, the knowledge of what is happening will make things easier for everyone with you.

May you be blessed with grace and peace,

Lectra

When I finished reading, Gaius said, "The men who continue these searches don't know exactly who they're looking for. The interest in Codros has evaporated, but the story about you, Thekla has grown to unimaginable proportions. Some claim that you're ravishingly beautiful and others say that you bear scars from being attacked by beasts. They know there's a woman who teaches a new religion in public markets so they're scouring public areas."

"Thank you for bringing the letter and telling us what you know. Although I taught in the market here last week, we're preparing the grotto so that I can teach here. People will need to choose to come here rather than stumbling on me teaching in the market." Thekla said all this in a quiet voice, clearly disturbed by the news of how innocent people were being affected.

Gauis looked concerned. "Did something happen?"

She smiled and shook her head. "No. When I began teaching in markets with Paul, I was dressed as a man. This was the first time I tried to teach dressed as a woman. There were no problems, but I wasn't comfortable."

"We discussed the possibilities that this property offers for Thekla's work and are nearly finished making a new path to the grotto," Codros said. "Acca and Daphne are helping Thekla make the cave more comfortable, Soon, she'll begin teaching there."

"We can show you what we've done tomorrow. Perhaps you will have some ideas for us," Pallas said.

The men were gone most of the day and returned to villa toward evening. Covered in dirt and sweat, it was apparent that they'd all been working hard. I waited until we were eating that evening to find out what they'd been up to.

Codros wiped his mouth after drinking deeply. "Gaius had a good idea for making the entrance to the path more secure. Instead of a direct route to the meadow, he suggested that we add a few turns to slow down people as they approached. There's one spot where someone can observe people as they arrive without them being aware of us."

Thekla's hands flew up, palms outward, as if that could halt activities. Her eyes narrowed and her face flushed in anger. "That's going too far. I don't want people to be spied on when they come here."

"The spot doesn't have to be used, but it offers the possibility of some security if these reward-seekers try to find you. I'm sure you have friends in Seleucia who can let you know if it's necessary to be alert for the troublemakers," Gaius continued, unaffected by her outburst. "Besides, we know that they accost innocent people and you would not want those coming to see you to be seized."

Pallas looked at Thekla. "Maybe you should see what we've done before you get too worried."

Codros took the lead by walking out of the front gates to the main road. From there we turned left and then entered the new path. We had gone a short distance when the path swerved to the right around a natural mound and what appeared to be a natural rock formation between some trees. Codros stopped and pointed at the boulders.

"We moved the rocks together yesterday. There were several scattered around this area. By moving them carefully, we were able to create a formation that looks like it has always been here." He motioned for us to follow him.

The way the stones were placed behind the boulders, someone could sit unnoticed with an easy view of those walking on the path.

Gaius said, "This spot doesn't have to be used, but it's available if you ever need some security."

Thekla walked up and down the path and all around the boulders. Finally, she nodded her approval. "But, we'll use it only if we need to."

Gaius stayed with us a couple more days before heading home. He promised to share our news with Onesiphorus's family.

A few days later, all of the work in the grotto and cave had been finished. Codros and Pallas carved the outline of a fish in the bark of several trees so people would recognize the path. I decided to accompany Thekla on her first day of teaching. We approached the grotto using the narrow path from the villa, and heard women talking quietly seated in groups of twos and threes. When they saw us, conversation stopped.

"Welcome. This is where I will teach from now on," Thekla said and extended her arms to include the entire grotto. "You will be able to meet me here whenever you want to discuss the new faith."

I looked at the people who had come, mostly women and a couple older men. They had spread cloths on the ground and judging from the sacks of food and skins of water, it appeared that they were prepared to stay for a few hours. Thekla sat on the boulder that Codros had placed below the ledge in front of the cave entrance.

She raised her hands and prayed, "Father and Mother God, thank you for this opportunity to be together and for this beautiful day." She paused for a few moments in silence and then looked at the group. "Last week I spoke in general terms about the new faith way. Today,

I'll tell you part of my story and how I came to be a believer," Thekla said.

Seated in the back of the group, I could hear her clearly. There wasn't a whisper; even the rustling stopped. The only sound aside from Thekla's voice was birdsong.

"As a young woman, I first heard Paul speak when I sat at the bedroom window of the villa where I was raised in Iconium. I was searching for something more without knowing what I was looking for. Paul taught that a man called Jesus lived with love and forgiveness for everyone. Paul said that this was the way all human beings were intended to live as children of divine parents. I was amazed when he said that Jesus allowed himself to be crucified and forgave the soldiers who nailed him to the cross as he hung there. Mystified by such behavior, I stayed at the window and listened to everything he said, but was thirsty to know more. My mother wanted me to stop listening to him and she brought the man I was betrothed to, hoping to break the hold these new teachings had on me. They connived to have Paul arrested, but that didn't stop me. I decided that I had to hear more and went to see him in prison."

I scanned the group listening intently to Thekla. Unlike the people from the market, these people had chosen to come hear her. They did not interrupt or call out as she spoke, but sat with family members or companions. I recognized many from the marketplace when she first spoke. Then, they were dressed in soiled clothes, having just stepped away from their stalls. Now, they wore brighter colors and were prepared to stay for hours with baskets of food and jugs of wine arranged by their sides.

"We talked through the night. Paul told me about his personal encounter with the risen Jesus as he traveled to Damascus. My mind and heart opened wide to receive the new teachings. I knew that this was the way I wanted to live my life. The following morning, I was arrested too and kept in the same cell that had been Paul's. My punishment was to be burned because I fled my fiancé and refused to be married. They feared that if I were unpunished, other young women would break their marriage contracts.

"Once the wood was prepared in the market square, they tied me to the stake and started the fire. The smoke billowed around my head and I coughed, but suddenly it began to rain in great torrents. People who had come to watch the spectacle, ran for shelter. Strong winds tore apart awnings and anything loose. I didn't feel afraid, because I knew what Jesus had done with his life and death. Suddenly a mighty bolt of lightning struck the edge of the square with instantaneous thunder. I knew then as clearly as if a voice had spoken that I needed to go to Paul."

Thekla paused and poured water from the skin she had brought with her. When she finished drinking, she looked at each one. "Paul told me about the Spirit, the Holy Comforter that Jesus sent to guide believers. When I mentioned my experience with the thunder, he told me that the Spirit could communicate with believers in many ways and if I continued on the path of faith, I would recognize the Spirit's guidance. In the weeks that followed, I understood that what Paul said was true. The Spirit communicates with anyone who is willing to listen and learn about the new faith. When you open yourself to these teachings, the Spirit comes to you and you are transformed. Your outlook on life and your behavior change. By your desire to be here and listen to me speak, I believe that you are opening your heart and mind to a new way of living."

Everyone's attention was riveted on Thekla's face which radiated joy. She smiled and again looked carefully at each woman who'd come to hear her. "Do you have questions?"

"What about marriage? Why did you run away from your future husband?" A young woman asked in such a quiet voice that everyone leaned toward her as she spoke.

"Marriage is not wrong. Paul and I believe that it is important for each one to determine the priorities that are right for his or her life. Making this commitment to live with love and forgiveness can be very demanding. I could not travel or teach if I were married with children. It may be possible for some parents to consider this, but I am not able to. I've dedicated my life to teaching the new faith way and have vowed to remain celibate."

Thekla's posture was not as erect as it was when she had started; she appeared drained.

"Let's take a break," I said. "In the future, you will always be able to meet Thekla here. She is eager to share all that she knows about the new faith with you. This is the first step to a new, gentle way of living."

Thekla gave a quick nod of agreement and added, "Come here any time you want to learn more. I will be here every day."

When she climbed the narrow path to the cave, I followed her. I fixed some bread and fruit for us and sat with her as she stretched out to rest.

We all settled into the new routine, with Acca and me taking turns going with Thekla to the grotto each day. Codros and Pallas maintained the path. We often talked about the grotto and Thekla shared reactions from the visitors. Word spread and the number of people coming to hear her expanded. Being nestled below the cave and surrounded by trees, the grassy area where people sat to listen to Thekla was protected from strong winds and rain. Regardless of the weather, Thekla went to the cave every day.

We'd been so involved with our normal activities at the villa and helping Thekla at the grotto that none of us had gone into Seleucia for a several weeks. Codros often helped me with the garden when he had a chance. I enjoyed his companionship and his advice about the gardens. He was thoughtful whenever we were together, always looking for ways to make things easier for me. Even when we ate, he always passed me choice portions before selecting his own. I had never had someone care for me like this before. Even Abrax, after all of our years together, had not shown such thoughtfulness.

When Kittos and Crisa stopped late one afternoon, we were delighted to see them, but their manner was subdued and preoccupied. Kittos and Crisa exchanged a meaningful glance and she gave him an encouraging nod.

"Today some strangers came to the market looking for Thekla. They didn't know her name and couldn't describe what she looked like."

Crisa interrupted her husband. "We got concerned because they asked for the woman who taught in markets about the new faith. The way they searched all of the stalls with their swords drawn, they didn't seem interested in learning about the faith."

Codros gave me a meaningful glance, and said, "A friend came from Iconium a while ago and brought us the news that mercenaries were searching outlying areas and other towns for Thekla in the hope of receiving the reward for her capture."

"We will be alert for any sign of these men. Tell us what they looked like," Pallas said.

Before Thekla left for the grotto the next morning, Codros and Pallas searched the area for any sign of unexpected visitors. Once they were sure that no one was lurking in there, they worked out a schedule to keep watch over visitors from the hiding place in the boulders by the entrance. Acca and I continued to take turns accompanying Thekla to the grotto. Our vigilance remained high for the first week. Kittos and Crisa had not seen the mercenaries again. By the end of the second week, we relaxed and the men stopped guarding the entrance to the grotto footpath.

Our former routine re-established itself. We grew accustomed to Thekla's schedule and all took turns accompanying her to the grotto, often staying until she finished teaching.

Although the winter months were not as cold here as in Iconium, still the mornings were quite chilly. Rainfall kept everything damp. All of us had braziers in our rooms. We discussed adding one in the grotto cave for Thekla, but the temperature in there seemed to remain steady regardless of outside conditions, and it was always dry.

One morning I accompanied Thekla to the grotto carrying an extra blanket. I had become so accustomed to the path as it descended to the grotto, that I wasn't watching where I stepped. The blanket slipped and wrapped around my feet. The next thing I knew, I was flying head first into the grotto hitting, my legs on boulders and scraping my arms on stones next to the trail. That was my last thought until I opened my eyes in the grass to see Thekla's pale face. First she said a prayer and then she wrapped me in the extra blanket. One of the women who had been waiting to hear her came to Thekla's side. Her mouth moved as if she was speaking, but I couldn't make out the words. The woman knelt by my side and rubbed my cold hands as Thekla ran for help.

I must have dozed off because I woke up in my room snug in a pile of blankets with Codros at my side. When I tried to sit up, he put his hand on my shoulder and rearranged the pillows. I faded in an out of sleep all day. Most of the time, I woke to find Codros with me, but other times it was Acca who fed me rich broth. That night, they kept an oil lamp burning in my room. In the morning, Codros was half asleep on cushions he'd placed next to my bed.

Thekla wore a worried expression when she came to see me before going to the grotto. "How are you feeling?"

Every time I moved my head, it ached fiercely. "I'm just very tired."

"You hit your head on a boulder as you fell, and it knocked you out. Codros carried you back to the villa and has been with you most of the time since then."

I smiled. It was difficult to stay awake for more than a few moments at a time. Although the hours and days that followed blurred together, my periods of wakefulness lengthened and I could enjoy conversation again. I was most aware of Codros staying with me. A week later, I felt restless and he helped me move to a couch next to the windows in my room where I could see the gardens while Acca changed the sheets on my bed. It became our morning routine until I could get up by myself. Although I was improving, Codros was never far away and was attentive to any need I had. We didn't talk much those first few days, but he often held my hand as I lay with my eyes closed. It was reassuring to know that he was there.

Four weeks after my fall, I had regained some independence and was able to go to the gardens on my own. Codros knelt in the rows of vegetables pulling weeds. I headed for a bench in the shade and he looked up. He finished the part he was working on and came over to me.

"Welcome back to your gardens, Daphne," he said wearing a huge grin of satisfaction.

"Codros, I'm surprised to see you weeding. I thought this was one chore you disliked more than all others," I said.

He nodded. "It's true, but I know how diligent you were about keeping them under control. It bothered me to think of you spending more hours working here because they'd been neglected so I decided to work on them."

I turned to him intending to kiss his cheek, but he turned at the same moment and we ended up kissing each other on the lips. Our arms entwined around each other of their own volition, it seemed. When we finally released each other we were breathless. His embrace awakened sensations that I thought were gone forever after Abrax's death.

Codros looked into my eyes. "I was afraid that I would lose you."

I took his hand in mine and held it tightly. "We will not lose each other."

"I thought my life was over in Iconium, then Thekla came and everything has changed. I feel like a new person, with my life ahead of me," he said.

"When Abrax died, I thought that the possibility of loving someone had passed. I am so glad that Thekla brought us together." I stood up, still holding his hand, and we went to my room.

In my bedroom, he slid his arm around me and drew me close so that our bodies meshed together, and we kissed again. At some point, he picked me up and carried me to my bed. With great gentleness we explored each other before yielding to the urges that united us.

I must have dozed off and woke when I heard some one call Codros. When I opened my eyes he was smiling at me. He kissed me lightly and left before someone came looking for him.

As the days passed, the change in our relationship was apparent to everyone. They seemed happy for us, but I worried that Codros and I needed to find another place to live.

The first time I was alone with Thekla, I asked her, "Would it be better if Codros and I left the villa to find a place of our own?"

Stunned by my question, she asked, "Why do you think you have to leave us?"

"But, I thought everyone who lived here was supposed to remain celibate."

Thekla smiled and shook her head. "For those who want an intimate relationship and promise to stay committed to each other, there is no problem. No one is required to be celibate. The teaching is that both ways are acceptable. You and Codros do not have to leave, but when you're ready, we should have a ceremony to bless your relationship."

I hadn't thought that far ahead, but what Thekla said made sense.

A week later, we held a feast and invited Kittos and Crisa to be with us. Before Acca served the food, Thekla asked everyone to meet her in the grotto. Kittos and Crisa exchanged a puzzled look because we hadn't told them about the blessing. Codros and I decided that we would arrive last. As we entered the grotto, the others were standing waiting for us. Thekla beckoned for Codros and me to join her at the boulder where she usually taught.

"Friends, we are meeting here to bless the relationship between Daphne and Codros. There is no preference for us in the way we live our lives, whether celibate or married, except that we be true to our commitments to the Spirit and to each other. Is there anything you want to say to each other?"

Codros faced me and looked into my eyes as he said, "Daphne, I am committed to your well-being and will love you for the rest of my days."

Taking his hand in mine, I said, "Codros, I will stay faithful to you and committed to your health and happiness for the rest of my life."

Thekla smiled and raised her hands above us all saying, "Before our Divine Parents we recognize Daphne and Codros as husband and wife and ask that their lives be blessed."

Everyone clapped. Thekla embraced me and then hugged Codros. Acca and Crisa hugged me too. Pallas and Kittos slapped Codros on the back and hugged him. Acca hurried back to the villa to serve the food.

I overheard Kittos say to Codros, "You are a very lucky man, for all that you have been through to enter this time of your life with such a lady."

I don't know what Codros may have said because Pallas congratulated me and kissed me on the cheek.

Back at the villa, Acca had outdone herself with the feast. She had asked Kittos and Crisa to bring some of their wine and fruits that we did not have at the villa. It was a delightful afternoon. For the first time all of us could be together without worrying about projects that needed to be undertaken or other serious issues.

Crisa asked, "Will you register your marriage with the city?"

Codros and I exchanged a look. Although it had been over a year since the last bounty hunters had come to the market, Codros and I decided that we didn't need to have official sanction of our relationship on public records. "We've decided to keep our names off the registry as husband and wife," said Codros. "At this time in our lives it's too late for a family." He extended his arms to include everyone and continued, "This is our chosen family. The law exists to protect offspring so there is no need for us to register."

The Second Year

It was hard to believe that it had been over two years since Thekla had moved to Seleucia. The villa had been fully repaired, the surrounding grounds were finally cleared of brush, and all of the fruit trees had been pruned. The gardens were thriving and required minimal maintenance to keep them going.

Acca suggested that we have a special dinner to celebrate when the four of them first arrived at the villa. Her delight was preparing meals and this dinner was spectacular, with a roasted pig on a spit. Codros dug a fire pit near the garden. Our good friends Kittos and Crisa would join us for the meal providing the pig. The garden had yielded vegetables by the basketful and there were a few herbs to enhance the flavors. The work Pallas and Codros had done with the fruit trees gave us a regular harvest of luscious citrus fruit, even the olives seemed bigger than before.

After the market ended, Kittos and Crisa arrived. Codros and Acca had started the roast hours earlier and we sat together waiting until it was done. No business or serious concerns would be discussed tonight. Wine flowed and a spare room had been set up for Kittos and Crisa in case they decided to stay overnight.

Codros and I sat together. It had been almost a year since Thekla blessed us. Our relationship more than filled the void left when Abrax died. My life was richer than it had ever been. I was content.

Now when I looked at Thekla, I saw a gracious woman who had matured rapidly as she took ownership of the villa and expanded her teaching role in the grotto. Her daily routine included meeting with people individually as well as teaching groups about Jesus's way of love and forgiveness.

The challenges that life brought to each us of seemed to be re-solved for the time being. We were a very content group, aided by good food and wine. Kittos began singing and soon all of us joined him. I hadn't sung in years, but remembered many of the tunes from my childhood. When the singing ended, we cleared the remnants of our feast. Kittos and Crisa agreed to stay with us for the night.

Acca and I still accompanied Thekla to the grotto a couple times a week, but the need for extra vigilance finally had passed. Luxurious calm had descended on the villa. Each of us pursued our special projects, with Pallas getting very involved in orchards. Codros usually puttered around the villa keeping everything in good working order. Acca delighted in feeding us and I was thrilled with the way the gardens met our needs for vegetables. There was some discussion of buying a clutch of eggs so that we would have our own chickens.

The only shadow on my happiness was the problem of recurrent headaches which often kept me in bed for several hours and sometimes the entire day. Codros always fussed over me and I enjoyed his attentiveness. But I would much rather have been rid of the headaches. The general opinion was that they were due to my fall in the grotto.

We hadn't heard from anyone in Iconium for months. According to Gaius, the bounty hunters didn't know who they were looking for anymore, but hoped to get lucky. The temptation of easy money made them careless. Now they demanded ransom, regardless of whom they seized. At last Iconium's governor intervened and forced Theokleia to withdraw the reward. I suspected that too many upstanding people had been harassed and detained.

One morning Thekla went to the grotto alone, earlier than usual. She returned quickly accompanied by a woman wrapped in a damp palla with twigs caught in her brown hair. Strain showed in her face with deep furrows across her forehead. She glanced around quickly and lowered her eyes rather than look directly at any of us. Her fear was palpable. We all gathered in the courtyard as Thekla introduced her to us.

"This is Chloe. She came here looking for a safe place to stay and had hoped to remain in the grotto. In return, she asked if there was some way that she could help me." One by one, Thekla introduced each of us to Chloe. "Chloe has told me part of her story and I'm sure that she will tell us more later. Chloe's husband died recently and being childless, his family threw her out. Her parents have died so she has no home to return to."

Acca reacted immediately and looking directly at Chloe, said, "You can stay here. There's plenty of room."

Chloe's eyed widened and she said quietly, "But you don't even know me."

"None of us is family by birth, but we live together as a family by choice. You would be welcome."

I turned to Chloe. "Acca and I can show you around the villa so that you can choose a room for yourself. I'm sure that we can help you find what you need. Each of us has shouldered some of the chores to take care of the villa, orchards, and gardens. You may find that there are chores you'd like to do."

Thekla had been watching Chloe as we talked. "Would you like to stay with me and my friends?"

Chloe nodded as tears spilled over her cheeks. Thekla hugged her. She was such a frightened and timid creature. I hoped that given enough time, she would blossom into the woman she was meant to be. When Acca and I took Chloe on a tour of the villa she chose a room on the second floor, next to Thekla.

Since Codros and I had merged our rooms, we had duplicates of many pieces of furniture. I took Chloe with me to see what she might like. Acca scurried to a storage area in the back of the villa for sheets and curtains. Codros and Pallas moved the furniture upstairs for Chloe. She spent the afternoon arranging the room.

When we met for our evening meal, Chloe was missing and Thekla went to her room where she found her asleep on the couch. After dinner, while the men were talking with Chloe about the orchards. Thekla told Acca and me that she'd seen cuts and bruises on Chloe's legs.

We accompanied Chloe when she went to her room and offered to bandage her legs.

At first Chloe denied having any injuries, but then she sobbed and lifted the edge of her long toga. Some of the cuts were deep and infected. Where her legs weren't cut there were dark bruises. Acca filled a basin with warm water. We tore old cloths into strips to cover the deeper wounds.

"How did this happen, Chloe?" Acca asked in a gentle voice.

Chloe's face flushed with embarrassment. "My husband cut his leg when he felled a tree. He wouldn't let me care for it until it became too painful to move. By that time it smelled awful and oozed all the time." She shuddered and wiped tears from her cheeks. "Despite all that I did to try to care for him, his leg swelled and turned black. Soon after that he died. My father-in-law beat me claiming that I wasn't diligent enough to cure his son. He came to our room the next day with his sons and chased me out of the house with a whip. I couldn't pick up anything, except the few things I normally carried with me. As I scurried away, he shouted, 'Don't come back or I'll kill you for the loss of my oldest son."

I took Chloe in my arms and held her as she sobbed quietly.

"You are safe with us. No one will harm you here," Acca said.

We stayed with Chloe until she was settled in bed and falling asleep. The others were waiting as we went back to the atrium. Acca told them Chloe's story.

"I suspected something like that," Thekla said. "When I found her in the grotto, she winced as she stood up and limped as we climbed the path to the villa. I was sure that she had some injuries, but didn't want to ask too many questions then."

Codros gave me a knowing look and said, "She'll heal quickly here. Pallas and I offered to show her around the orchards tomorrow. After hearing about how she was beaten, perhaps Daphne should come with us."

I nodded.

Chloe was the first of several widows who came to live with us. Chloe and Acca worked as a team to get them settled comfortably in the villa and helped them adjust to our way of life. Whenever Chloe could get away from her new responsibilities, she went to the grotto with Thekla.

One morning, after finishing a few chores in the garden, I went to the grotto. I'd been writing about Thekla for a long time, but had never heard her teach in her permanent place. When she started teaching, I was always preoccupied with setting up her cave or other chores. The last time I had been there was the day I fell. I felt compelled to hear her speak without distractions.

If I followed the path we normally took to the grotto, I would disrupt her speaking because the path was visible to everyone and she might think I was coming to her about an urgent problem at the villa. I left through the villa's front gate and walked to the road where I could see the fish sign to the grotto path. As I walked I felt a new buoyancy and enjoyed the wild flowers that grew along the way. I approached the clearing and saw a very large gathering so I seated myself near the trees in the back and listened. Thekla's voice carried well and I could hear her easily.

"Welcome. Everyone in the human family is welcome. Do not be preoccupied with your past experiences. Whatever has happened in the past, whether good or bad, is over. What matters now is how you choose to live today, tomorrow and every day still to come." Thekla smiled and opened her arms to include everyone as she spoke.

I looked around and saw some shaking their heads and others

appeared puzzled by Thekla's welcome. She paused and observed everyone before continuing.

"There is nothing you can do to remove yourself from the human family. Our Divine Parents hold you tenderly in their care regardless of you faults, your social status or limitations." She paused again.

My thoughts veered away from the grotto to recall critical moments in the past. I had always tried to do my best, but wondered whether that was good enough, especially when I lived on the edge of society shunned for my occupation. Loud birdsong in the tree next to me drew me back to the grotto.

"There is only one unforgivable sin and that is to deny the existence of the Eternal, the Power that is beyond us all. When we refuse to accept that which is beyond us, we are totally lost because we are incapable of knowing the love of our Divine Parents.

"Human love is imperfect and incomplete. The love we know from our Divine Parents is full and encompasses every fiber of our being. It is unconditional and unending."

As she spoke I felt saturated with love. I was like a piece of bread that had been dipped in wine and had soaked up more than it could hold. I felt so full of love that I wondered if it could leave traces in my footsteps. I remained suspended in love without a care for my surroundings. I didn't hear or feel a thing except for the total awareness of love.

A person jostled me as they left the grotto and I regained a sense of my surroundings. I didn't want to leave. Then, Thekla joined me.

"Daphne, I'm so glad you came," she said reaching out to hold my hand. "You've worked so hard since you first came that I thought you would never be able to spend time in the grotto."

I hugged her. "Today, for the first time, I fully understood your teaching. In the past, I've heard the words as a pleasant discussion, but today I felt them."

Tears streamed down Thekla's face. "You are the most important person to me in this world. I have hoped that one day you would understand this new way of living. Your face tells me that all of your hesitancy and doubts have been erased."

We remained in the grotto until people began to return for the afternoon discussion. I knew that everyone would be anxious when we did not return for the noon meal, so I took the short path back to the villa.

The first person I met was Chloe bringing a basket of refreshments. How she had changed since the first time we saw her. Now she walked confidently with her head held high. She radiated contentment. She spent as much time with Thekla in the grotto as she could. If she could skip all of her commitments, I knew she would spend each day in the grotto with Thekla.

As the number of the people living in the villa continued to grow, assisting Thekla could become Chloe's only responsibility. The new women had already assumed some of Acca's chores so that she focused her efforts on preparing our meals with the produce from the orchards and my gardens supplying most of our needs.

My Task

Headaches were coming more frequently, but Codros assured me time and again that it was part of the recuperation from the fall. The last time I tried to write, I couldn't focus my attention on the words I wanted to write. My thoughts seemed garbled and wouldn't flow as they used to. I got angry with myself and quit writing. Tears of frustration poured down my cheeks. Codros told me to be patient with myself, but the pain got worse and there was no improvement. Discouragement seized me.

Seated at my desk at the window, I stared at the blank page unable to begin writing. My frustration mounted. Then, I thought of the first time I sat down to write about Thekla. I was frustrated then too because no one would accept my commission to write her story. How I struggled to find words to begin. After many false starts, I became comfortable with the task and the words began to flow. My favorite place to write had been in my courtyard in Iconium. There was so much to record and I wrestled with revealing my own life as I wrote about hers.

When she first became involved with Paul and then Queen Tryphaina, I thought our relationship would change. But, the bond between us was secure. We learned more about each other and my respect for her deepend.

In Seleucia, the story has changed, or my approach to it has lightened. I no longer feel anxious about writing. In the past, I always feared for her safety and thought each page might be the last one. Now that she's safe, writing had become more enjoyable than before.

Writing has become more difficult and the flicker of joy has faded. I have assessed each of the women who have come to live with us in the hope that one of them might take over my task of recording Thekla's life, but none of them is literate nor does anyone demonstrate any interest in learning. There was a time when I thought that Pallas might assist me, but he has so much work in the orchards that I cannot impose on him. Perhaps someone will come who can work with me.

Harvest season has come to a close. Acca and I have stored all of the produce from the gardens. What we weren't able to use, we gave to the people who came to the grotto to hear Thekla. She and Chloe had gotten to know those who come regularly to hear her speak and who needed the surplus from our gardens for their families.

When we first made the suggestion, Pallas and Codros were opposed to giving the vegetables away and thought that we should sell them in the market. Their primary concern was that hoards of people would come directly to the villa in search of food. Once we determined how to distribute the produce to those in need, they acquiesced. Chloe made parcels that were given out at the end of the day in the grotto. Some bartered their services or offered items they made. No matter how much we gave away, we never experienced need in our large household.

Surprise Visitors

Thekla and most of the women were in the grotto after our break at midday. Acca and I were clearing the remains of our noon meal when Pallas hurried back into the courtyard.

He grinned and said, "We're about to have visitors."

"Who is it?" Acca asked.

With a twinkle in his eyes, he returned to the front gate calling to us, "Wait and see." Then he waved to Codros to come along.

Acca and I looked at each other and stopped putting away food in case the visitors needed refreshments. We ran out to see who had come. In front of two horses and a heavily laden pack horse, the men from our villa greeted the two who had just arrived.

Onesiphorus gripped Codros in a bear hug. A familiar tall young man was shaking Pallas's hand. Zeno. No longer dressed in the short toga of a youth, he was taller than his father. I looked around for Lectra, but saw only the two men.

Onesiphorus saw me searching for the rest of the family and said, "Lectra and Simmias send their greetings to everyone. She wasn't able to come with us and Simmias stayed to help her. Hopefully, the whole family can come on our next visit."

Zeno helped Codros unload the horses while Onesiphorus accompanied the rest of us inside. We sat under the corner tree where we had just finished eating.

"What's the news from Iconium? Pallas asked.

Onesiphorus frowned. "There's not much to tell. The ruling council has put a stop to the random searches for escaped criminals and slaves. Now our household has a calm routine that hasn't been possible for years. The new governor forced Theokleia to withdraw her bounty for capture of Thekla and Codros."

Most of the time, we forgot about any lingering threat for Thekla or Codros. Thekla was so busy with her responsibilities in the grotto that she seldom left the property. Only Pallas and Codros went into town when there was an essential need that we couldn't supply from the resources at the villa. Nevertheless, the news released the tension that had surfaced as soon as we saw Onesiphorus and Zeno.

"On the whole, things are going very well. Paul wrote that more house churches are being established throughout the region. He asked me to check on some activities in Tarsus. Since Seleucia is on the way, Zeno decided to accompany me this far. Lectra is working with some new women who've joined our household and asked Simmias to stay and help her organize a room for them along with some other pressing needs." It seemed as if he wanted to say more, but didn't.

After dinner that night, Zeno looked around at everyone. He cleared his throat, and said, "I have known for a long time that I have been led by the Spirit to work with Thekla. I'm not sure what kind of task I am meant to do, but I want to live here with all of you."

For several moments, no one said a word. Thekla, was the first to respond. "Of course, you are welcome to live here. I know that when the Spirit leads someone to a new task, it takes time to see the path clearly."

Zeno looked directly at Thekla and said, "I want to be more like Paul and work to spread the news about the new beliefs, but I am not a traveler or a gifted speaker. I have learned a great deal from my parents about maintaining a house church and I'd like to do that work here."

"When you are married, you can bring your wife to live in the villa too," Thekla said.

Shaking his head, Zeno answered, "I don't think that married life is the way for me and I've asked my father not to arrange a marriage contract for me."

Everyone turned to Onesiphourus who seemed sad and subdued.

"Our family has discussed Zeno's future for months. As soon as he came of age, I tried to interest him in a betrothal, but he resisted. Finally, Lectra and I understood that his life would be different from what we imagined. We are glad that he has kept this new faith and are content that he has chosen to come here to live and work."

"For as long as you are meant to be here, we will be happy to have you with us, Zeno. Tomorrow Pallas and Codros can show you around and give you an idea of the routines we all follow. Perhaps that will help you find the work that suits you most," Thekla said.

Onesiphorus had work in Seleucia and Tarsus and left soon after breakfast the next day promising to come back before heading home to Iconium. Pallas suggested that Zeno spend a day with each of us to learn about our roles in the household.

Just a week after Zeno's arrival, it seemed as if he had always lived with us. One day, he asked to work with me. I thought he was interested in the gardens and we spent a lot of time outside, until my head throbbed so much that I needed to rest.

"Daphne, go inside. I'll finish weeding the garden," Zeno said.

His offer to finish the chores was welcome, but as I stood up a wave of dizziness made me fall. He caught me before I hit the ground and guided me to my room. After I was seated on the bed, he said, "I'll find Codros for you."

I nodded and laid down. When I opened my eyes it was late in the afternoon and Codros was with me. I didn't join the others for our evening meal, but continued to rest. It took me several days to feel strong enough to resume my regular routine. Now Codros or Zeno always worked with me.

Zeno passed by my living room one day as I was writing about Thekla. When he stopped, I invited him to join me.

"I don't know many people who write," he said. "I thought most of the writing was done by scribes."

"Do you know how to write?" I asked.

"Well, yes. Everyone in our family writes, including my mother. Having a house church for new believers as well as maintaining my father's business we found that it was better if all of us could write," he said.

"Most upper class women can read the languages of our region, but few have the chance to learn to write. I learned as a young woman so that I could keep my own records," I said.

Zeno tilted his head to the side in thought. Then he asked, "Do you keep accounts for the villa?"

"No," I smiled and shook my head. I passed the vellum I was writing on to him and watched as he read what I had written.

He raised his eyebrows in surprise as he read. "You're writing about Thekla."

"Since she was first arrested in Iconium, I've been writing about her life. Initially, I tried to hire scribes to do the work, but they just laughed at me for wanting to record the life of a young woman. That meant there was only one person to do it, me. Unfortunately, since my fall a couple years ago, it has become increasingly difficult to work. I get headaches so quickly that I can only work for a short time."

Zeno looked at the page in his hands and then turned his attention to me. "I'm still looking for the things I could do here. There's nothing in particular that needs a second person at the moment. Both Codros and Pallas have the orchards and buildings under control. Would it help if you could dictate to me whatever you want written down? I could become your scribe."

As he spoke, it felt like a huge weight was being lifted from my shoulders. "Oh, yes. That would help a lot. Should we try working together tomorrow after I finish my chores in the garden?"

Zeno smiled. "I could do more in the garden too, if you show me what to do. After that's finished we can work on Thekla's story."

From then on, we often worked together whether in the gardens or writing. Spending so much time with Zeno, Codros teased me that I had a new boyfriend. Our routine went very well and I was soon up to date with Thekla's story. Zeno and I shifted our routines to working more in the gardens and only twice a week to write. I was glad that we had made such progress because the headaches had become much worse and I often needed to rest much of the afternoon.

One day, I fell asleep immediately after our noon meal. Codros woke me in time for dinner.

He held me in his arms and looked into my eyes. "Daphne, it was hard to wake you up. I've noticed that you're sleeping a lot more. What's happening to you?"

"The headaches have been getting worse. The only thing that gives me relief is to take a nap. Today, the pain was particularly vicious. Zeno does most of the work in the gardens now." A tear slipped down my cheek. It made me so sad to explain the changes I was experiencing, especially to Codros. I'd been hoping that with enough rest, I would feel better, but I was getting worse.

"We should talk to Thekla," he said, then kissed my forehead before helping me to get up.

The next morning, Codros brought Thekla to our rooms before she went to the grotto. By the expression of concern on her face, I knew that Codros had told her about my increasing problems.

"I wondered why you had not come to the grotto in such a long time. Now, I understand." Thekla took my hand and held it in both of hers. "You've been in my prayers because I've missed your companionship."

She placed her hands on my head and prayed, "Spirit, your will is done in all things. We are grateful for all that Daphne does. I treasure her like a mother. If it be according to your will, ease her pain and renew her strength."

Codros's face was covered with tears at the end of her prayer. As Thekla left for the grotto, he came to my side and sat with me.

At the door, Thekla turned back to us. "Daphne, I know you've worked very hard in the garden for months. Why don't you let Zeno take charge of them and act as his assistant whenever you have the energy? I know you love the gardens, but he needs to find a place here. Your headaches may be the sign that it's time for him to take over."

I nodded. "He's been doing the majority of the work now. It makes sense for him to take over as long as I can be involved as I'm able."

Codros chuckled. "You won't be able to stay out of the gardens completely, but you always enjoyed figuring out what to plant when. That's something you can do easily when you're seated in that shade. I'm sure Zeno needs your guidance on the best way to manage the gardens through the seasons."

This plan worked very well and the headaches subsided. I was able to relax and appreciate everything that Zeno did with the plants. He had an aptitude for nursing plants when they needed extra attention or to be transplanted to better location so that they could thrive. As the months passed, the gardens and shrubs responded to his attentiveness. He cared for each one as if it were special. By harvest time the yield was abundant.

On occasion, I knelt and helped pull weeds or pick produce, but my role now was more an advisory capacity. Zeno often asked for my advice before making any major change regarding which vegetables we planted and the best locations for them. I felt very satisfied with the role reversal we'd made regarding the gardens.

The twice weekly routine of writing together continued unchanged. Zeno was a willing scribe and had a very readable script.

"Zeno, have you had time to explore the grotto and Thekla's cave?" We had been working together and he seemed confused about the orientation of the path leading to the grotto, its lay out and the cave extension.

He shook his head. "I didn't want to interrupt Thekla. When I arrived, I assumed that I would be working with Pallas or Codros so I didn't pay much attention to Thekla's area."

"Maybe you should go with her tomorrow and see how she works. I think you might understand some of the things that I'm trying to describe there as well as her schedule. She is very gifted in the way she works with the people who come, both individually and in groups. While her teaching is derived from what she first learned from Paul, your mother has told me that her style is very different."

He smiled. "The harvest is in and there is not much to do in the gardens so it's a good time to take a break from those chores. I'll check with Thekla to be sure it's all right with her."

Zeno spent several days exploring the vicinity of the grotto and listening to Thekla teach. While he was occupied there, I ambled through the gardens and pulled some weeds when they popped up. The growing season had passed so there wasn't much to tend to, but I enjoyed being around the plants. Codros had placed a bench in the arbor next to the gardens so I often rested there until noon.

Codros joined me at the bench and slid his arm around my back. "You look happy and more well rested than I've seen you in a long time."

"I feel good. Zeno has done such a good job with the plants and I enjoy being outside to admire his work. I didn't realize how much of a burden the gardening had become until I turned it over to him," I said.

"I was worried when he arrived," Codros said. "He's so young and active that I wasn't sure that he would fit in or find enough work to keep him busy. I'm glad that he's relieved you of the hard work. He has adjusted so well to our routines in the villa, that I tend to forget that he wasn't with us from the very beginning."

Alone in our room, I looked at the scrolls I had written about Thekla and breathed a sigh of relief. Zeno also had adopted my approach to writing about her with a very clear script that can be read easily. I felt that I could release this task to him in the knowledge that her life will be remembered long after I'm gone.

A Great Loss

C odros walked into my room carrying Daphne's wooden chest of scrolls and writing supplies. Grief had etched deep lines in his face that made him appear much older than when I first arrived seven months ago.

"Daphne would want you to continue the work she did both in the gardens and writing about Thekla's life. She liked you a lot, Zeno, and enjoyed working with you." Codros said looking for a place to put the box.

I took it from him and said, "Daphne was a remarkable person. She was always kind to me and my brother when we were young. Since my move to the villa, it felt like she was a member of my family."

Codros looked down at the floor as his eyes filled with unshed tears. He nodded and left. I looked at the chest of scrolls and felt a weight on my shoulders. It seemed impossible that I could continue her work alone. Daphne is gone and there's no one else to complete Thekla's story.

Six weeks ago, Daphne was walking alone in the gardens as was her custom each morning. Just before our midday meal, Codros went to the garden to sit with her and found her lying, breathing but unresponsive, on the ground. He shouted for help as he carried her to their rooms. Acca was the first to get there. She helped him get Daphne to bed and called one of the other women to fetch Thekla from the grotto. Thekla and I ran back to the villa together.

Thekla ran directly to Daphne. She glanced at Codros whose attention was riveted on his wife and unaware that we had arrived. She prayed, "Holy Spirit, we are grateful for Daphne and ask for your blessing on her life. Guide us to care for her and help her return to her daily routines. Above all, we pray that everything be done according to your will." Thekla took a seat next to Daphne across from Codros.

Daphne remained alive but unconscious with Codros at her side. Thekla, too spent most of her time with them. Whenever she had to attend to other duties, one of us stayed with Codros as he watched over Daphne. Acca brought trays of food for whoever happened to be with Codros and Daphne while the rest of us ate in the courtyard.

Five days later, just before dawn, Codros shouted her name and we all ran to him. He held Daphne in his arms and kissed her as tears ran down his face. When he was able to release her, Thekla, Acca and some of the other women bathed her now lifeless body and wrapped it in a linen cloth.

Pallas and I stayed with Codros. When he regained his composure, Pallas asked, "Where should we bury her?"

At first Codros seemed dazed and unable to understand. We sat together in silence for a long time.

"There's another smaller dry cave in the hill above Thekla's grotto. It would be good for her to stay close to Thekla," Codros said so quietly that I could hardly hear him.

"I know the place," Pallas said. "Do you want to come with us to prepare it or should Zeno and I fix it for her?"

"I'll try to help, but I can't leave her yet," Codros replied.

Once the women had finished, Codros returned to the room they shared. Pallas led me to the cave he and Codros had chosen. We took a different trail and cut branches to widen the path for others to follow later. Creating a better walkway took all morning so we returned to the villa to eat and gather other supplies for clearing the cave and making a resting place for her body. Pallas talked briefly to Codros before we left and asked, "Do you want to carve the resting place for her or should we do it?"

His eyes were puffy and red, but his tears had subsided. "I'll fix the place for her. Let me collect the tools I want and I'll join you."

I was glad that we had worked on the path first because it was easier to carry all the things we needed. We were nearly at the top of the hill when Pallas made an abrupt turn to the right and disappeared. There was no ledge in front of the cave which would make entering while carrying Daphne very difficult. He and I cleared a small area and created a step into the entrance. As we finished, Codros arrived bearing several chisels. I lit a torch and we went into the cave together. Codros walked around the walls and stopped at the back of the cave. He picked up a chisel and carved a line about waist high. Once the place was well defined, Pallas and I helped him hollow out a shelf. We lost track of time, until we heard someone calling us. Chloe carried a lantern to show the way on the new path.

Pallas and I went out to meet her, surprised to realize that night had fallen.

"Acca asked me to see if you will be coming back soon for dinner?" Chloe asked as she peered into the cave where Codros still worked.

"Ask her to keep some food out for us and we'll return as soon as we've finished here," Pallas said.

She passed him a full jug of water before leaving. He quenched his thirst and passed it to me. I carried it inside to Codros, who paused for a drink.

He was making a very elaborate shelf to hold Daphne's body. There was no ornamentation, but a depression that would almost caress her body with a slight elevation for her head. As he finished, Pallas and I swept the debris from the cave.

At dawn, we formed a procession to the cave. Codros led the way, followed by Thekla and the rest of the household. I was surprised to see Kittos and Crisa from the town market join our procession carrying two rose bushes. When we arrived at the cave, Codros tenderly placed Daphne's body in the place he had carved for her. Tears streamed down his face. Thekla stood next to him and turned toward the rest of us.

"Daphne led a full life. She was gracious to everyone she met regardless of their status in society. She was like a mother to me and I am deeply grateful for her life." Thekla paused for a long time and looked at each of us to see if anyone would add to her comments. No one spoke.

"The teachings of Jesus reveal that life is unending. While Daphne is not with us in a physical form, she goes on in a life we cannot yet know. Like unborn chicks inside the egg, we know only this world, but nothing of all that is in the life to come. She has been welcomed to continue in eternal life not only by the Holy Spirit, but also by those she has loved in the past: her parents, her mentors, my father, and others." She turned to Codros and said, "Your loss is profound, but Daphne did not abandon you. You will come to know her more fully in her absence and rejoin her when your work in this life is completed."

She raised her hands to encompass all of us. "Eternal Mother and Father, we give you thanks for Daphne's life. Bless Codros as he learns to live in a new way each day without her by his side. Bless us all as we each give thanks for the time we knew her and continue to learn to live in the new faith. May it be so, amen." She dropped both her arms to her side and reached out to caress Daphne's body before leaving the cave.

Each of us went to Daphne's side and said our silent good-byes while Codros remained standing near her head. Many returned to the villa, but Codros lingered. When Kittos and Crisa left the cave, they planted the rose bushes on either side of the entrance before returning to the villa. Pallas and I waited to close the cave and accompany Codros.

I looked at the chest of Daphne's writing and wondered how to proceed. Perhaps, if I read what she had written I would be able to write the rest of Thekla's story. I picked up the first scroll and read silently.

"The day that had started with such beautiful weather now bore down on Iconium with intense wrath as it approached midday..."

Discussion Questions

1. Prior to reading about Thekla what ideas did you have about women's autonomy in the first century? How have these thoughts changed?

2. Hetaerae were a professional group of respected women in Greece. This role evolved in Ancient Greece to provide highly educated courtesan escorts for men. Were you aware of such a role in ancient times? What do you think of a role like this for women?

3. Jesus's first language would have been Aramaic. Translating the New Testament to English from this language offers a broader of understanding than we are accustomed to. How does the use of personal pronouns (he, she) affect your understanding of God and/or the Holy Spirit?

4. In your experience, how does religion describe the impact of the Holy Spirit today and how might that be different from earlier times?

5. Metanoia can be defined as a transformative change of heart in an individual. Is this kind of transformation still occurring today? If so, how have you seen it unfold in yourself or others?

Additional Reading

The list below is in chronological order and spans a wide arc of topics that were useful to me and provided tremendous insight to the cultures and setting of the first century as well as the religious controversy about Paul and the role of women in the early church.

Academic and Religious Studies:

<u>Apostle Paul</u>

Dennis Ronald MacDonald, *The Legend and the Apostle* (1983). He explores the true identity of Paul as a first century apostle and the legends surrounding Paul's work including the legend of Thekla.

John Temple Bristow *What Paul Really Said About Women* (1988). This work studies the traditional understanding of Paul's teaching, especially the view that he is unsympathetic to women.

John G. Gager, *Reinventing Paul* (2000). The author examines issues and controversies surrounding Paul's teachings, especially the way that he refuted the teachings of Jesus's disciples. Gager's work focuses particularly on the New Testament letters to the Romans and Galatians.

<u>Role of Women in the Early Church</u>

Elizabeth Schussler Fiorenza, *In Memory of Her: A Feminist Theological Reconstruction of Christian Origins* (1983). She offers a detailed search for women's involvement with early Christianity by examining the books of the New Testament.

Ross Shepard Kraemer, *Her Share of the Blessings* (1992). This work explores women and religion during the Greco-Roman period focusing on pagan, Jewish and Christian activities. A discussion of Thecla is included in "Autonomy, Prophecy and Gender in Early Christianity"

Karen Jo Torjesen, *When Women Were Priests* (1995). Torjesen documents the roles of women in the first centuries of Christianity as priests, bishops and prophets. She identifies the historical documents that demonstrate leadership activities of women.

Jean-Yves LeLoup, *The Gospel of Mary Magdalene* (2002). This is an English translation of the Gospel of Mary with notes and commentary.

Karen L. King, *The Gospel of Mary of Magdala* (2003). King presents the Gospel of Mary and discusses the teachings of Jesus in her gospel. She presents the framework of Mary's teachings during the first century.

Scott Fitzgerald Johnson,_*The Life and Miracles of Thekla* (2006). This work is a literary analysis in which he examines basic information about Thekla in the context of Greek literature.

Novels:

Anne Rice, *The Vampire Chronicles*. This series includes twelve novels published from 1976 to 2014. Her writing focuses on issues of belonging, immortality, and the distinction of good versus evil. Published in 2001, *Blood and Gold* provides wonderful descriptions of the cultures and architecture in Rome and Antioch during the first Century.

Elizabeth Cunningham, *The Maeve Chronicles*. These books were published from 2000 to 2013 and includes a series of four novels exploring the life of Mary Magdalene and her relationship with Jesus during his teenage and early adult years that are not discussed in the New Testament. She provides in-depth description of cultural practices and beliefs from Celtic lands in the British Isles to Asia Minor during the early decades of the first century. Her work explores the significance of the divine feminine during those times. I found *The Passion of Mary Magdalen* and *Bright Dark Madonna* to be particularly insightful.

Acknowledgments

This book would never have been written without the prompting given by Susan C. Sims who caught the excitement I felt about Thekla's story the first time I mentioned her. Susan worked tirelessly to help me develop and polish this fictitious account about Thekla based on the account of her life in the "Acts of Paul and Thekla" on the internet. Others who were essential in providing suggestion and insights for crafting the tale include readers who critiqued the manuscript as it was being written: Sandy Cody, Jerri Glover, Becky Luther, and Leslie Wey. More than the comments, the support of these people kept me going as I explored the best way to tell about Thekla's life.

I extend my deepest thanks to everyone who helped make this book a reality.

CPSIA information can be obtained at www.ICGtesting.com
Printed in the USA
BVOW05s0232210316

441120BV00001B/96/P